# SNOW

GALAXY ALIEN MAIL ORDER BRIDES: A
QURILIXEN WORLD NOVELLA

## MICHELLE M. PILLOW

MICHELLE M. PILLOW® - MICHELLEPILLOW.COM

Galaxy Alien Mail Order Brides: Snow © Copyright 2018 - 2019, Michelle M. Pillow

First Electronic Printing January 8, 2019

Published by The Raven Books LLC

ISBN 978-1-62501-220-3

**Alpha male alien comes to Earth to pick up a bride and instead meets a beautiful scientist whose job it is to capture him.**

*NYT Bestselling Author, Michelle M. Pillow, is back with a brand new sci-fi alien romance adventure.*

Tushar (aka Snow Chaos) knows there is little chance of finding a wife on his ice-ball of a home planet. Few can survive the subzero temperatures. When Galaxy Alien Mail Order Brides offers to introduce them to women eager for love, he and his brothers can't resist, but Earth is far from welcoming.

He knows he should focus on getting home, but all he can think about is laying claim to the sexy scientist who works for the bad guys.

Jennifer works for the Milano Foundation in an attempt to undermine their efforts. When Snow and his brothers land, it's like a dream come true for her diabolical alien-kidnapping coworkers. Now she has to make a choice--keep her cover, or betray a dangerous corporation to save the alien she's falling in love with.

Snow might be a blue humanoid from another planet, but life with him might be worth the risk.

WELCOME TO QURILIXEN

QURILIXEN WORLD NOVELS

## Dragon Lords Series

Barbarian Prince

Perfect Prince

Dark Prince

Warrior Prince

His Highness The Duke

The Stubborn Lord

The Reluctant Lord

The Impatient Lord

The Dragon's Queen

## Lords of the Var® Series

The Savage King

The Playful Prince

The Bound Prince

The Rogue Prince

The Pirate Prince

**Captured by a Dragon-Shifter Series**

Determined Prince

Rebellious Prince

Stranded with the Cajun

Hunted by the Dragon

Mischievous Prince

Headstrong Prince

**Space Lords Series**

His Frost Maiden

His Fire Maiden

His Metal Maiden

His Earth Maiden

His Woodland Maiden

**Dynasty Lords Series**
Seduction of the Phoenix
Temptation of the Butterfly

To learn more about the Qurilixen World series of
books and to stay up to date on the latest book list
visit www.MichellePillow.com

## AUTHOR UPDATES

To stay informed about when a new book in the series installments is released, sign up for updates:

michellepillow.com/author-updates

# WELCOME TO GALAXY BRIDES
## A NOTE FROM THE AUTHOR

Dear Readers,

For those of you familiar with my bestselling series, Dragon Lords, you've already been introduced to the Galaxy Brides Corporation and the services they offer lonely men and women of the future. What you might not have known is that Galaxy Brides (formerly aka "Galaxy Alien Mail Order Brides") dabbled in taking grooms to destinations—namely Earth! Unfortunately, they found the alien males a little too hard to control once they landed on our surface.

I hope you have as much fun reading this series as I've had writing it!

Happy Reading!

Michelle M. Pillow

GALAXY ALIEN MAIL ORDER
BRIDES

HAVE YOU READ THEM ALL?

Spark

Flame

Blaze

Ice

Frost

Snow

PRAISE FOR MICHELLE M. PILLOW

What readers are saying about the
Galaxy Alien Mail Order Brides series...

5 Stars! "Hysterically funny, spicy and sweet."

5 Stars! "One of the best alien romance stories I have read!"

5 Stars! "A must read to all who enjoy alien hotties!"

5 Stars! "Action, Intrigue, and humor with a happy ever afters!"

5 Stars! "Funny, adventurous, and romantic. The male aliens are funny as all get out!"

*To the Pillow Fighter Fan Club*
*A big thanks to dedicated readers like you willing*
*to help spread the word about the books they love.*
*Thank you!*

## PROLOGUE

*Planet of Sintaz*

Tushar heard a loud creak and looked up from where he prepared fur to sew a winter cloak. No part of the hunt was wasted on the ice tundra planet, and he had several more hours worth of work before he finished. Otherwise, he would have gone out to greet the landing spaceship with his brother, Edur. Even if it were a traveling sales craft, a conversation with someone who wasn't related to him would be most welcome.

Life on Sintaz was hard and lonely. Not many people could survive the harsh weather. Tushar lived with his two brothers in a modest ice hut.

Their home was furnished with three stools, three beds, three chairs, three bowls. They never had visitors, and anything that was not needed or used would be considered wasteful. After their parents had died in an ice storm while hunting, it was just the three of them—Izotz, Edur, and Tushar.

When they were younger, there had been a village, but his neighbors had begun migrating off world. Some went to find easier work in cold storage ships. Being Sintazian made them particularly adapted to working in freezing temperatures. Others had joined up with the Exploratory Science Commission.

The ESC scientists drilled core samples out of the tundra in what was estimated to be the beginning of a hundred-year-long mining endeavor to penetrate fifteen-thousand feet below the planet's surface to test mineral compounds. He wasn't sure what they thought to find by going through thousands of years worth of compressed snow, ice, and ships that had crashed on the planet. His people told stories of the alien spacecrafts beneath the ice. If the myths were true, perhaps it would be worth digging.

Tushar heard another loud creak and dropped his tools. It sounded like the metal of a ship. He stretched his arms, walking across the ice hut to watch the ship leave. The day was warm, so he didn't wear a shirt. Aliens who visited the planet bundled themselves head to toe. He'd laugh at them, but knew his own body was not suited for hot climates. He was biologically adapted to the environment.

A loud crack preceded the unmistakable sound of an ice avalanche.

His smile dropped, and he rushed through the front door. Outside was a frozen stretch of terrain filled with snowdrifts and ice patches. Pieces of ice sprinkled from above, clinking on the ground around a rather large pile of broken ice that had not been there before. A ship disappeared into the sky.

Instantly, he realized what had happened. The idiots had landed in a snowdrift which had melted a little but then froze to the hull of the ship, and then broke off during takeoff. If not for the danger to those standing below, it would have been funny.

By the size of the pile, the ship was lucky. There were places on the surface which could swallow a craft whole. Ships landing in them would be so buried in snow that they'd become one of the many legends beneath the ice.

Tushar saw blue amongst the white. Edur was in the process of pushing up from the ground. Dark blue blood dotted his back, indicating he'd been hit by ice shrapnel. The minor wounds would heal quickly in the cold and were not life threatening.

"What did the alien ship want?" Tushar asked as he walked down the path to where his brother stood. The aliens had not stayed long. He peered over the icy landscape to see if any visitors had stayed behind and determined they had not. His attention paused on the chunks of ice that had fallen from the sky. Either they left the new mound outside their door permanently, of he'd be hauling it off later. It was too much to hope that it would melt away on its own.

More to himself than his brother, he muttered, "It's warm today. Izotz will want to hunt for the winter supply."

"Merchants." Edur held something in his hand. Tushar wondered at his brother's expression.

"Snowsuits or heat dispensers?" Tushar

laughed. Aliens were always trying to sell them things they didn't need.

"Women." Edur's lip twitched. "They want to marry us off."

Tushar threw back his head in laughter at the joke. Oh, how he wished it was a ship full of women looking to marry them. "Wouldn't that be something, a bride procurement agency landing here for the three of us? They'd probably try to pair us with those hairy aliens we saw with the ESC. Who else could withstand our temperatures?"

"Or Izotz's cooking," Edur joked.

The brothers laughed. Izotz was not the best in the kitchen which was amusing considering their local cuisine was limited to bearguar or bellaphant dishes.

"What were they selling?" Tushar asked again, more out of bored curiosity than a need to know.

"Women," Edur repeated.

At that, he crossed his arms over his chest and studied his brother. "No, really. Why won't you tell me?"

Edur lifted his hand to show him the metal disc he carried. It looked like a holographic sales chip. He handed it to Tushar. "They are looking to take men to Earth for mating."

Earth? Tushar had never heard of the place, but it sounded like some kind of Fajerkin fueling dock. That hardly sounded appealing—places where stranded alien females were looking to hitch a ride to whichever space port would have them. He studied the disc without turning it on. "What is Earth?"

"A planet with many women," Edur answered.

A planet? Tushar had to admit that piqued his interest...not that their older brother would ever agree to it. Izotz did not believe in leaving Sintaz for half-formed opportunities. This was the life they knew, and here, they were safe and free. No one was going to try to take over an ice settlement.

Edur's expression looked suspiciously guilty as he took a deep breath, refusing to meet Tushar's gaze.

"It sounds like the women are expecting to be abducted, and are even excited about it," Edur said.

"What did you do?" Tushar placed a fist on Edur's shoulder, forcing him to meet his eyes.

"I signed us up to go." Edur almost sounded

scared to admit the truth. "They took my space credits. I do not think I can get them back."

Tushar stood still for a long while as he processed the information. A trip like that would not be cheap, and he imagined paying for three passages had wiped out his brother's account. It's not like they needed money, but space credits did come in handy when it came to ships selling things they could actually use, like food and weapons.

Tushar let his hand drop from Edur's arm and looked toward the hut. Izotz was resting on his bed after spending the last two days tracking a herd of migrating bearguars. He must have been in a deep sleep not to be awakened by the ice crash.

"You signed our brother up for a marriage trip?" Tushar clarified, holding back his amusement. "Izotz? On a spaceship? To this *Erd* place?"

Edur gave him a hopeful grin. "Will you help me convince him of the idea?"

Tushar couldn't contain himself as he began to laugh. There was no way in all the universes he was going to tell Izotz they were flying to an unknown region with an unknown procurement company to look for unknown women to mate. He shook his head in refusal. "No."

Edur did not look surprised by the answer, even as he asked, "Will *you* go?"

Tushar laughed harder. It became difficult to breathe. This was the funniest thing to have happened to them in a long time. "It depends on how hairy these *Erd* brides are, but first I want to see you tell Izotz he's to be married to an off-world hairy alien." He gasped for breath. "He is going to drop you down an ice crevice."

"The women are not hairy," Edur defended his choice. "They are..."

A hazy expression crossed over Edur as a small smile formed. He reached for Tushar's hand with the disc and then tapped it to begin the holographic commercial. A blue and brown planet appeared, the somewhat transparent orb rotating above Tushar's hand. The image of white clouds drifted around it. There appeared to be a bright light source coming from space though he couldn't see it.

"It looks...warm," Tushar said for lack of a better word.

Edur nodded at the device, indicating he should watch and listen.

Tushar lifted it slightly.

A soft alien voice spoke in a foreign language,

only to be overpowered by a louder, deeper male voice that translated the words into Sintazian. "Is yours one of the many stagnant civilizations without enough women to produce offspring? Do you come from a monogamist culture with no one to marry?"

Edur again nodded enthusiastically as if answering the device.

"Or a polygamist culture in need of more food makers? Are you lonely and looking to reassign your assets?" the translator continued.

It was no surprise that its words were a bit of a jumbled mess. Sintazian was a hard language for people to grasp the nuances of, and the aliens who programmed the translators had yet to perfect it. Most likely because, compared to the rest of the galaxies, there weren't many who spoke the language. The brothers had dealt with enough visitors to become fluent in bad translations.

"What if we told you there is a planet whose name is called Earth that could solution all your needs? Would you be jolly? Earth has women they are willing to share. So, join us for jolly-making on Earth, where all your humanoid female fantasies can become digestible food."

Edur reached to pause the recording. "I think

that is a bad translation. Bob did not indicate that we are to eat the Earth women."

Tushar frowned. "I should hope not. Who's Bob?"

"He is the alien I spoke with about the trip. He works for a corporation called Galaxy Alien Mail Order Brides. It is all very official," Edur assured him. He again turned on the recording and gestured that Tushar should watch.

"Earth has a breathable sky, food you can put in your heart, and..." The translator gave a small error tone, as if it couldn't translate its own message, and began chattering in a rapid succession of indistinguishable words before resuming, "officially discovered life forms not of their own planet but are humanoid compactible and ready for travel to their new homes."

Again, Edur stopped it. "I don't think they mean for us to compact them."

Tushar frowned. "I speak bad translator," he assured his brother before resuming the hologram's message.

"Upon mate selection, all necessary papers will be given to the Earth government and transport will be taken upon us, as you leave the planet with your new food makers, we will provide the transport. Those wishing to stay on Earth will be provided with manly identity."

The image of a female alien appeared before him.

Now *that* got his attention. Tushar studied the figure intently. Though strange in skin tone, she had arms and legs. She wore skintight clothes. Her hair fell long down her back in brown waves. Her body curved a little in the midsection, but not enough to be unpleasant. He paused the image to get a better look. Two round globes protruded from her chest.

"What are those for?" Tushar pointed.

"I don't know." Edur poked his finger at the image. It distorted but then righted itself. "I'd like to find out."

"Interesting," Tushar whispered. He turned the hologram back on and suppressed the desire trying to vibrate through his body.

"I thought so," Edur agreed.

"Option one," the translator said, still turning the image.

"Option two," the translator continued, as the holographic image of a second Earth female appeared. This one had light hair piled high on her head and clothes that sparkled. The third option wore dark goggles around her eyes though he wasn't sure why she would need protective eye gear for the object she read from. It hardly seemed dangerous. Her hair shade was closer to the Sintazians' black. Option four had red hair and breathed smoke from her lungs. She too had curves.

"This last option is my favorite," Edur said, sounding very much like a boy who'd just had his first successful hunt.

"Option five," the translator said.

Tushar could see why. A female appeared with little in the way of clothing, except a piece of cloth over her chest mounds and a second clinging to her hips. Her hair was not one discernable shade but several.

"I would like to vibrate inside her," Edur said.

Tushar nodded, agreeing with his brother's candid remark.

"That is all of them," Edur said in disappointment.

"It does indeed look like this *Erd* has women," Tushar agreed. To his surprise, he realized he wanted to go. He knew nothing about this corporation or this planet, but if they produced a mate, he was all in.

"Well?" Edur asked. The hologram turned, showing the date they were to leave. "Will you come?"

Tushar tried to hide his eagerness. The last woman he'd vibrated in had been an ESC scientist. She had wanted little to do with him other than bending over so he could place himself inside her. The arrangement had not been one of love, but who was he to say no to a willing partner? It ended poorly though when he discovered she also bent over for the hairy Lykan she worked with, and a Dokka trader who was as green as Tushar was blue.

"If you get Izotz to agree, yes, I will come to *Erd* with you."

His wanting to go didn't matter if they weren't all three on board with the idea. They could not leave Izotz alone on Sintaz. It would not be safe.

Edur smiled in determination. "I'll convince him. I have to. This might be our only chance to find wives." Then grinning wider, he added, "Can you imagine having someone every night?"

Tushar could imagine. It wasn't just the vibrating, it was the idea of having a woman committed completely to him, and he to her. It was the idea of children and a bigger family.

"Put that away for now," Tushar said as he handed back the disc. "Prepare the weapons. I'm going to finish with the fur before we go."

Edur nodded, but the smile did not leave his face.

DECEMBER, NORTHERN MINNESOTA
WILDERNESS, SEVERAL EARTH
MONTHS LATER...

EARTH.

The planet was nothing like Tushar had expected. Galaxy Alien Mail Order Brides had severely misled them when it came to Earthling females' readiness to be abducted, and it became quickly apparent upon landing that most of the population didn't even know aliens existed. They had been dropped off on a primitive globe whose inhabitants had not yet ventured past their own little piece of space.

Earth technology in many ways was childlike. Their movies created unrealistic fears of the unknown. In fact, most of the storylines were laughable. Why would an alien want to conquer such a planet? Yes, it sustained life, but so did a lot of other places that were situated in more advantageous locations.

Tushar realized he might be a little bitter. They'd been on Earth for months, and he was the only brother left without a wife. Izotz, who hadn't even wanted to come in the first place, found Elle right away. Sure, she was part of the mercenary team that had kidnapped him upon their arrival, but she was also the reason he was now free from that same group.

The Milano Foundation had sent mercenaries to wait for them when they'd first landed. Initially, Tushar thought they had been betrayed, but it turned out Galaxy Alien Mail Order Brides was just incompetent. Galaxy Brides wanted so badly for this business endeavor to work, and they had no problem cutting corners to make it happen.

Tushar trudged through the snow, enjoying the crisp air. Galaxy Brides had given them medicine that reacted with their body chemistry to change their skin from blue to human-toned. After the Milano mercenaries had come for them a second time—kidnapping Tushar, along with Elle and Ice—he'd stopped taking it.

Oh, and that's what he was supposed to call Izotz now, Ice. Ice Storm Chaos. Edur was now Frost Chaos, and Tushar's Earthling name was Snow Chaos. They were assured these were strong, sexy human names. Snow was beginning to have his doubts.

What was the point of trying to blend in? It's not like there were any women around to mate. Snow wasn't sure he wanted a woman who'd care about the fact he had blue skin.

Even if there had been a way to meet more women, there was no guarantee they would want him. He'd met several in Colorado when he'd been trying to find a way to free Ice the first time. None had been interested in him. And he wasn't interested in them.

Sure, he could have easily vibrated inside a few, but sex was not love. He wanted love.

Seeing his brothers happy made his loneliness bearable. He would give up everything for his family. Ice with Elle, and Frost with Meg, that was worth protecting. So, he hid in the wilderness near the Northern United States border. Meg's stepmother, which apparently was some kind of human custom of mating a second time, let them stay on her family property. No one bothered them in the old cabin. The structure was much more conducive to human survival than a Sintazian ice hut.

Snow was used to the isolation of being away from settlements, but now he felt as if he didn't have his brothers to talk to. They were busy with their wives, always whispering, kissing, and vibrating. There were only two bedrooms, so he slept alone on a small couch. And apparently, Earth women didn't like when you walked into their bedrooms, so he had no one to talk to at night when he couldn't sleep.

Plus, they made him wear clothes all the time. Human females had odd notions when it came to nudity.

That is how Snow found himself in the lovely cold night air, wearing only boots and boxer shorts. The snow crunched beneath his feet, the sound oddly comforting as it reminded him of home. It was about the only thing that did. Trees lined the dark path he walked. The barren limbs stretched overhead, outlined by moonlight to create strange shapes. They stirred feelings of foreboding inside him.

"I am Tushar of Sintaz," he whispered in his

native language, just to hear the words. "This planet has many women, but none for me."

"Hello?" a voice whispered. "Is someone there?"

Snow frowned and wondered if he should answer. No one was supposed to know they were out here.

Footsteps crunched through the snow and then paused. "Hello?"

This time, he could hear the softer tones in the voice. It was a female.

"Okay seriously, if someone is out here, know that I am armed and not afraid to—"

Snow stepped toward her, the sound of his movement cutting off her words.

As he came to a place where the trees opened up to allow the moonlight in, he found a woman bundled in winter clothes. He couldn't see much beyond the red hair poking out from her knitted hat. A black scarf covered her chin and partially buried her mouth. Shadows hid her eyes so he couldn't see them. She stood beside a camera that had been propped up on a stand.

Snow instantly went to the device. It pointed in the direction of his home. He would not allow her to expose them.

She made a small noise of protest as he grabbed it, stand and all. "Hey, stop, that's mine."

"Now it is mine. I cannot allow you to…" He frowned as he followed her eyes to his chest. He wasn't wearing a shirt, and the blue of his skin would have been noticeable. He waited for her to panic.

Strangely, she didn't.

"Can't allow me to what?" the woman demanded.

"Take pictures of my family," he said.

"I'm taking pictures of the night sky." She pointed a finger upward.

"That makes no sense. Why would you walk out here in the cold to take pictures of the sky? You can take those anywhere." Snow did not release the camera.

"You're not an artist, are you? Now give that back to me." The woman reached her hand for the camera and gestured for him to hand it over. She was a little thing, and her attempt to command him did not frighten him.

What was an artist?

Snow tried to place the word from the uploads Galaxy Brides had put into his brain. They had been inserted to help him learn English and acclimate him for life on Earth. "No, I am not a person who draws or paints as a profession."

"Then what do you do, besides hate the arts?" she asked.

"I do not hate art," he protested.

"Just photography?"

"No, I—"

Her laughter cut him off. "I'm teasing you."

"Why?" He frowned.

"I'm trying to joke around to lighten an awkward situation," she said. "It's not every day I find myself alone in the forest, in the middle of the night, in the middle of winter, with a man in his boxer shorts. So who are you? What do you do?"

"I'm a..." Snow tried to think of how to answer. "I was a hunter at my old home, for meat. Then, when I first came to this land, I worked as an enforcer, for money to buy meat."

"Enforcer?" Her smile faded, and she took a step back. "Like for the mob?"

"No. In Colorado," he corrected, "and only for one man, a street king, not a mob."

"But you hurt people?"

"When they did not pay what they owed, I was sent to collect it." Snow hadn't minded the work. It was easy, and his boss hadn't asked many questions so long as he'd collected the Earth cash for him. He wasn't sure why more people didn't do it. Asking people to pay what they owned seemed honorable enough. It was honorable to pay one's debts. Who was he to question Earth's bill payment systems?

"Why are you telling me this?" She continued to inch away from him.

"You asked what I do." He watched her. Her expression was hard to decipher under the scarf and hat. "Now, you tell me, why are you out here? Why are you watching my house?"

"I'm not watching you. I'm..." She again pointed upward. "Winter nights are the best times for taking photographs of the sky. It's a hobby. I'm not making it up. When the air is cold it doesn't hold as much moisture, and so it allows for a clearer picture. I come out here because it's possible to get brighter pictures of the stars away from town. There is less pollution and alternative light sources like streetlights and houses."

Snow continued to study her carefully. She was trying hard not to look at his chest. "I scare you?"

"I'm in the middle of the woods at night with a half-naked enforcer who has painted himself blue and just stole my camera," she said. "Of course, you're scaring me."

Paint. That is why she wasn't freaking out about his being an alien. She assumed he'd painted himself. "Then why don't you run?"

She pushed her head back to nudge the scarf down with her chin, to show more of her face. Her cheeks lifted as she smiled, but the expression was tight and didn't automatically make it to her eyes. "Because you look like you could catch me, and I'm hoping you realize I'm not a threat."

Snow wanted to believe her. He glanced up. "You like stars?"

"I like the..." She sighed, her breath coming out in a cloud. "I like the possibilities that the stars represent."

When he looked down, she'd come closer.

"What do you mean?" he asked.

She gazed upward. "Imagine everything that is out there."

Snow didn't need to imagine. He knew what was in space—endless planets, some fueling docks, aliens. "You mean aliens?"

"Aliens, planets, black holes, time slips..." She gave a cute little laugh. "I sound crazy."

"You believe in aliens?" He detected a new

smell that did not belong in the forest and leaned closer to her. It came from her body.

"Yes." She looked at his naked arm. Snowflakes began to fall around them. "How are you not cold?"

"I'm used to this kind of weather."

"May I have my camera back?" She reached to take it from him. Her fingers brushed his, but he didn't let go.

"What do they call you?" he asked.

"What do they call you?" she countered.

"Snow."

She shoved her gloved hands into her pockets and bounced a little. "Nice to meet you, Snow. I'm Jennifer."

"I am sorry, Jennifer, but I cannot let you have the camera." He placed his fist against her shoulder in a gesture of goodwill. "I hope you understand."

Jennifer nodded. "I do." She pulled her hands out of her pockets and reached for his arm. He felt something prick his skin. "And I hope *you* understand."

His vision blurred, and he blinked as he looked down to where she'd touched him. Jennifer pulled a syringe out of his arm. She stepped back.

24

"Why?" Snow dropped to his knees.

Jennifer caught her camera before he knocked it over. Her voice was barely audible. "Because you weren't supposed to..."

Snow fell toward the ground.

W ELL, THAT COULD HAVE GONE BETTER.

Dr. Jennifer Petals looked at the alien on the ground. Being who he was, she wasn't worried about getting him out of the snow. It's not like she could have lifted him on her own, anyway.

She gave a little laugh. Snow. Who the hell was naming these poor guys? Spark, Flame, Blaze, Ice, Frost, Snow... The ridiculous list went on. It sounded like alien strippers had invaded Earth.

Looking down at the fit body beneath her, she sighed. The wetness of the snow started to seep into his boxers, adhering the material to his skin as if to reveal the sexy hip beneath. Alien strippers wouldn't necessarily be a bad thing. They were pretty to look at.

Jennifer pulled off her gloves and went to the bag she'd stashed by a tree. Tossing the gloves inside, she took out a cellphone. She pressed a contact labeled "grandma" and waited as the phone rang. A deep male voice answered, "Grandma here. Want some cookies?"

"Ugh, Jim, stop being weird," Jennifer answered. She knew for a fact that her twin brother had her listed in his phone as "angry ex don't pick up." People in their line of covert work tended to be snoopy by nature, and she didn't want anyone to know they were related. The less the Milano Foundation knew, the better. Sure, the records were there if anyone thought to look, but they gave them no reason to. Jim wasn't part of Milano. Jennifer had infiltrated the foundation all on her own.

They might have been born a few minutes apart, with Jennifer being older, but they couldn't have been more dissimilar in appearance. Jim looked like their mother, with dark hair and eyes. Jennifer took after their father's side, with red hair, brown eyes, and what the family called a fiery Irish temperament—even though she was only one-quarter Irish.

*Had* called a fiery Irish temperament. After her cousin had died in a plane crash, she and Jim were the only immediate family left.

"What's the status, Jenn?" her brother asked, suddenly sounding all business. "Are they all three there? Did we find them?"

Jennifer looked at the alien on the ground. For all his claims of being some kind of mafia enforcer, he came off more like a gentle giant. "I'm not sure."

"Then why are you calling?" he demanded in concern.

She sighed.

*Dammit.*

"Change of plans. I need to be picked up. One of them was walking the woods and found me. I tried to get out of it, but he didn't look willing to let me go, and I was running out of lies." Jennifer nudged Snow with her foot, unsure how long the substance she'd given him would keep him unconscious. Alien biology was unpredictable, but the reaction to TRQ-30 in the laboratory indicated it would incapacitate at least for a short while. This was her first time using it in the field. "I'm assuming the other two are nearby, but I have not gotten visual confirmation. I think we need to go in hot before they realize Snow's gone."

Jim whispered something away from the phone, and she couldn't make it out.

"Shit. This night just keeps getting better and better," Jim drawled sarcastically. "We have another problem. Big Papa is coming to town."

"When?"

"Just received word that his private jet filed a flight plan. He's on his way to Montana first thing in the morning." Jim grunted. "Guess he wanted to see why all his employees were fucking things up."

"Okay." Jennifer took a deep breath. "This changes nothing. We have no choice. Bring everything you got. We're doing this tonight."

"Hot and fast. Hang tight." Jim hung up on her.

Snow's hand twitched, and she tensed as she watched his face. Even though he was no longer listening, she whispered, "Jim, I need you to hurry."

Jennifer quickly glanced around to make sure Snow's companions weren't approaching, but she couldn't keep her eyes off the unconscious alien for very long. When Milano had held Ice at the facility, she had seen the video feed of him fighting. Gentle giant or not, they were strong.

She crouched next to him, balancing her weight on her feet to keep from sitting in the snow. Each of her breaths came out in white puffs. Snow's did not.

Curious, she reached forward. She'd never touched one of his kind before. His skin was firm and cool to the touch. She pressed her hand down flat. His two hearts beat a fast rhythm against her palm. Jennifer studied the markings on his shoulder, unsure if they were tattoos or some kind of birthmark. She traced them with the tips of her fingers.

Once the others came, she wouldn't be left alone with him again.

She had expected a lot of different feelings when she captured him, but not the one she was actually experiencing—attraction. It was more than his handsome face or kind eyes. As a scientist, the blue did not bother her. It was only a genetic abnormality; well, not abnormal for him, but for Earth.

Jennifer glanced at her camera. If he had

looked at her pictures, he would not have found stars. She'd been hunting the area, trying to locate the three extraterrestrial visitors. And she wasn't the only one.

Milano's mercenary assholes were also searching for them. He'd put a big price on the aliens' (*any* aliens') heads, and money made people do crazy things. She wasn't one-hundred percent sure what Milano's deal was, but she could guess it had something to do with rumors of his crackpot grandfather who swore he'd been abducted. The case had been famous in the 1940s and a public embarrassment to the powerful family. The stories still came up when anyone searched their name on the internet.

Realizing Snow's chest had stopped lifting with breath, she tensed and moved her hand over his hearts. They still beat. Her eyes darted up to meet his gaze. The second their eyes locked, he moved so quickly that he had her on her back in the snow before she could even think to scream. His weight pressed on top of her. He blinked as if he had a hard time focusing.

Jennifer had always been more lab geek than a fighter. Her only go-to move was to knee a guy in the balls and run. Right now, she wasn't in a position to do either. She felt a vibration along her hip and for a second thought it was her cellphone until she realized her phone was lying on the ground away from them.

"Are you going to answer that?" she asked, lacking anything better to say.

He kept her pinned down, but his eyes moved to the side. "You did something. What?"

Jennifer didn't respond. The longer she stalled, the better chance she'd have of getting her brother's help. He'd be tracking her phone for a location.

Snow made a strange noise, and it took her a moment to realize he was speaking in an alien language. Just as suddenly as she'd found herself on her back, she was hauled up and over Snow's shoulder. Her stomach bounced, and it knocked the wind from her for a moment.

When he began walking, she started kicking her feet and flailing her body to wiggle free. He held on tighter. At one point, she managed to buck up and back. It was a miscalculation as she almost knocked herself unconscious on a tree branch. He dropped her to the ground. Her feet bounced before he had her lifted once more. This time, she was cradled in front of him as he kept going.

Jennifer bit the inside of her mouth and resisted the urge to scream. This group of visitors was not known for aggression and only showed signs of it when trying to escape.

She couldn't be sure who else was in the woods. But she did kick at his legs, smacking him at an awkward angle a few times. Small noises of discomfort were the only indication that he felt the blows.

He brought her to a small cabin. The sight of it caused all reason to leave her, and she inhaled a deep breath, prepared to yell. What did she really know about these aliens?

The sound barely left her lips before he clamped a hand over her mouth to quiet her.

Snow brought her to the door and bumped it with his foot a couple of times. "I do not wish to restrict your breathing. Please stop."

She cursed at him from beneath his hand. The sound was a mumbled, incoherent declaration of anger. He kicked the door again. This time, someone answered, peeking through a crack.

"Snow?" Frost opened the door wider. "Did you lock yourself—"

Snow pushed his way inside, taking Jennifer with him. Her feet dropped to the floor, but he didn't release her.

"What have you done?" Frost demanded.

"What is happening?" Ice appeared in a doorway.

Jennifer stopped struggling as she tried to draw deep breaths through her nose. There was no reason to panic. Jim would find her phone and be able to follow the tracks in the snow easily. He'd come. She'd be rescued. This ordeal would be over soon.

"Our brother abducted a bride," Frost answered. "She's pretty but looks a little angry around the eyes."

Through the strands of hair hanging wildly over her face, she watched the two aliens study her. Their skin was blue. The last time Ice and Snow had been captured, they'd done something to disguise their skin color.

*Wait, did he say bride?*

Jennifer's eyes widened, and she reached to pry the hand from her mouth. She was aware of how close Frost's mostly naked body was to hers. The vibrating caught her attention again. It came from between his hips. That wasn't the only thing coming from his hips. There was the unmistakable feel of an erection pressing into her.

She knew from the scans Dr. Hanklen had ordered when they'd had Ice imprisoned that these men were human compatible. Hanklen was the head scientist in charge of Milano's pet project. He was also a giant asshole.

"She is not my bride," Snow said. "We cannot trust her. She lies."

The disappointment she felt at his easy dismissal stung. She wasn't sure why.

"What are you guys doing in here? Come back to bed."

Jennifer froze at the feminine voice, her fingers still attached to Snow's hand over her mouth. She recognized Elle. The woman had signed on as one of the mercenaries.

"She put something inside me," Snow said.

Elle's eyes met hers, and the woman gasped in surprise. "Dr. Petals? What are you...?" Her arms lifted as if ready to fight. Like most of the mercenaries, Elle had thought the job was a joke. Whoever heard of being hired to track down aliens from outer space?

Jennifer had been different. She'd known aliens were real when she'd taken her job. It was the whole reason she'd wormed her way into the foundation.

Ice glanced at his wife and hastened to stop her from attacking. His eyes narrowed as he looked at Jennifer's face, partially hidden by Snow's hand. "Snow, where did you go? She works for Milano, in the facility. Are there more of them out there?"

"I don't know. She put something inside me, so I brought her here," Snow said.

"What did she put inside you?" Elle's eyes darted around the room, the only indication she was panicked by Jennifer's presence. "Do you mean she injected you with something?"

Jennifer tried to speak, but the words were muffled.

"Snow, drop your hand," Elle ordered.

He listened to the woman. It was clear Elle had some kind of authority in the group.

"It's not what you think," Jennifer tried to explain. She pushed away from Snow and backed away from them. The door was blocked, so she edged toward a corner of the room. Moisture caused the boxers to cling to Snow's ass, and when he turned, his firm backside wasn't the only thing that was in full disclosure.

"What did you put in him?" Elle demanded. "Where are the others?"

"I need you to come with me," Jennifer said. This situation was out of hand. How could she make them trust her?

"Like hell," Elle shot. "You're not touching my family. Why can't you just leave us alone?"

"You don't understand. I'm trying to help." Jennifer could see they didn't believe her. She couldn't blame them.

A second woman came from behind Frost.

"Meg, stay back," Frost said, stepping in front of the woman. "Petals is dangerous."

"Petals are dangerous?" Meg asked in confusion as she yawned. She had a kind face and was the only one not staring at Jennifer in distrust. "What does that mean? And who's this?"

"Milano," Ice answered.

Meg's expression hardened. "What do you want?"

"We need to go," Elle said. "Tie her up. I'm sure her people are close behind. They'll find her and free her later. We need to leave. Now. Grab supplies."

"What?" Jennifer lifted her hands to stop any attack. "You can't do that."

"Would you rather I shoot you?" Elle quipped. "Because with the last several months I've been having, I can tell you I'm fine with that."

"No," Snow ordered. "You will not shoot her."

Elle furrowed her brow and then nodded once.

"She was alone in the forest," Snow said. "We are not shooting her with the Earth gun, and we do not have a blaster to incapacitate her that way."

"Yeah, I didn't mean a blaster," Elle mumbled.

"Actually, I do have one," Meg piped in. "I might have not-so-accidentally taken one when we were on the Galaxy Brides ship. After Bob shot me with..." Her words trailed off as if she wasn't sure she should be speaking in front of their visitor.

"You were on a spaceship?" Jennifer couldn't help herself. She always wondered about alien technology. There were reports from people who claimed to be abducted, but their accounts were highly suspect. In reality, flying in space wasn't an adventure she was up for. Heights terrified her. She couldn't even get on a plane without taking something to calm her anxiety.

"Get it," Frost told Meg.

Meg nodded and gave Jennifer a side-eyed glance before leaving the room.

"Trust me, none of Milano's people travels alone. I'm betting Dr. Hanklen is nearby, if she's here. Those two are always in the same location." Elle opened a cupboard in the kitchenette area and began placing cans of food on the counter. She called, "Meg, can you bring a bag for this food, please?"

"On it," Meg answered.

"And bring Snow some pants," Elle said.

"Way ahead of you." Meg appeared in the doorway and tossed a stack of clothes on the couch before disappearing again.

Snow didn't hesitate to take off his wet boxers in favor of a new pair. Jennifer tried not to look at his naked ass, but it was difficult not to peek. Then she found Elle staring at her from the kitchenette.

"What did you give him?" Elle finished taking out the cans, only to dig in the utensil drawers.

"A sedative." Jennifer pressed her back to the wall.

Elle bit her lip and nodded, then shook her head. She lifted her hands as her voice rose, "How can you work for them? Knowing what they are, what they do? They experimented on my husband. They put him in a cell, they beat him while he was chained up, you and Hanklen tortured—"

Jennifer stiffened at the accusation. "I never tortured."

"You're a part of it," Elle argued.

"So were you." Jennifer pushed away from the wall. "You're the one who captured," she gestured at Ice, "your *husband*. You're the only reason he was at the desert facility."

Husband. The idea would have been laughable if the situation wasn't so dire. Who would marry an alien to a human? How did a person even fill out that paperwork? Common-law marriage, maybe? Surely there would still be paperwork—

"Are you even listening?" Elle demanded.

"No," Jennifer said. Her eyes had strayed to Snow as he finished pulling on his clothes. "You do not seem to be in the place to have a rational conversation."

"Oh, there's the pompous Dr. Petals I remember," Elle scoffed.

The insult hurt.

Meg returned holding an empty backpack and

a metallic handheld device. She pointed the device at Jennifer.

It took Jennifer a moment to register what was happening. A blast of energy hit her stomach, and she looked at Meg in shock as her legs gave out beneath her.

## 4

Snow darted forward to catch Jennifer before she dropped to the floor.

"Ah!" Meg made a small noise of excitement. "I have always wanted to zap this thing." She then eyed Jennifer, and her expression fell a little. "Is she okay?"

"She'll be fine," Frost answered. "The same as you were after you were hit with the blaster."

Snow wasn't sure what to think about the beautiful woman in his arms. On the one hand, he wanted to vibrate inside her. (Fuck, how he wanted to vibrate inside her.) She was attractive, and she made every inch of his body react in favorable ways. On the other hand, she worked for the evil corporation threatening his family and had tried to sedate him.

Elle had worked for the same place, and she quit her job to rescue Ice.

What were the odds that Jennifer would do the same for him?

What were the odds she'd even care for him?

What were the odds he was grasping at dreams because he was lonely?

He adjusted her in his arms to better see her face.

What were the odds she'd let him vibrate inside her anyway?

"Snow, seriously?" Frost asked, his tone low. "This one?"

Snow realized he cradled Jennifer. One of his knees was bent as he knelt on the ground. Her legs sprawled along the floor as he held her behind her back and beneath her arm.

"What?" He pretended not to know what Frost meant. His body was pulsing loud enough for everyone to hear.

"You want to vibrate the evil doctor?" Frost gestured at Jennifer.

"No." It was a blatant lie told only to stop his brother's criticism.

"I can hear you." Frost gave a small laugh. "You always did like the... What do Earth people call them? Bad women? Crazy chickens?"

"Crazy hens," Ice corrected.

"Crazy chicks," Elle said. "And, Snow, you can't like the evil doctor. She wants to tie you up and experiment on you."

Snow couldn't help the small twitch that lifted the corner of his mouth. That didn't sound too bad.

"Men, human or alien, you're all the same—thinking with your little heads," Elle mumbled.

Frost and Ice kept their backs to Elle as they too tried to hide their laughter. Snow knew for a fact Elle had once tied up Ice in the bedroom. He wasn't supposed to know because humans were odd when it came to discussing sex, but his brother had been only too eager to share tales of the strange Earth female ways.

"I am not thinking with my little head," Snow said, "but with my two hearts."

"Oh, no," Elle declared, coming toward him. "No, no, no. You are not allowed to fall for Dr. Petals."

"I did not fall. I knelt." Snow adjusted her so that he could carry her as he stood.

"You can't love her," Elle insisted. "She's the enemy. Snow—"

"It is time for you to be quiet." Snow kept his voice calm even though he was aggravated. "You will not dictate the terms of my hearts. I am not yours to command."

Elle's eyes widened, and she took a deep breath. "You're right. I'm sorry for my tone, but I'm not sorry for the message behind it. You're my family. I don't want to see you thrown into a cage."

"That I will accept." Snow nodded. "Thank you."

"Food packed," Meg announced. "Go bags are ready."

"I'll get the car." Elle grabbed keys off the hook on the wall. Meg tossed her a coat on her way out the front door.

"Maybe we should take her." Snow held the woman in his arms, refusing to put her down.

"Like a hostage?" asked Meg.

"Maybe she will have knowledge that will help us," Snow insisted.

"Like a prisoner," Meg corrected herself.

"I don't think—" Ice began.

"I think it's a good idea," Frost broke in. "Bob

and Gary might be able to get information out of her."

"You think Bob and Gary can help? Those fools wanted us to move our women to Antarctica because Galaxy Alien Mail Order Brides is incompetent and should be out of business," Ice argued. "The North Pole is as cold as Sintaz. If that's the case, we might as well go home and lock them in a dome."

"At least on Sintaz, we do not have to fight that monster with the pointy-eared captives," Snow put forth.

Meg sighed and shook her head. "How many times do I have to explain Santa isn't real?"

"The information we saw was pretty specific," Ice countered. "There was a lot of documentation. Denying it will not make the threat to your planet go away."

Meg gave a small moan as she gave up the argument. "I'll find a ten-year-old to explain it you sometime." She gestured at the bag of canned food on the counter. "Come on, one of you strong men carry this heavy bag to the car for me."

"I will carry it," Frost said. "Someone grab the bags from my room, please."

"I will," Ice said.

Snow held Jennifer tighter. When Ice tried to shake his head in denial at Snow's attempt to carry her out the door, Snow frowned. "We cannot keep living like this, moving every couple of Earth months, hiding like we did something wrong. We need to end this once and for all, or we need to leave this planet and find a new home."

"I can't leave," Meg said, her expression worried. "My father needs me."

"I'm not leaving you," Frost assured his wife. "Earth is home."

Snow looked away from them. Watching his brothers' love for their wives made him want what they had. He tried to force himself to lay Jennifer on the couch but couldn't. He had not felt like this upon meeting any other Earth female. With Jennifer, something inside him came to life. What if she was his only chance at marital happiness?

His mind made up, he carried her out the front door to where Elle had a car waiting. There were not enough seats for everyone, but he could hold Jennifer on his lap.

He looked down at her unmoving face. Her arm flopped as it hung toward the ground. A tiny red light appeared on her shoulder, only to move up his chest.

He frowned, wondering what it could be.

"Snow!" Elle charged at him, knocking him to the ground. A loud pop sounded. He fell in a tangled mess of limbs. Jennifer didn't wake up. Elle rolled away from him and crawled through the snow toward the car. "Take cover!"

Snow hooked Jennifer around her chest, holding under her arms as he crawled with her toward the shelter of the car. Her body dragged in the snow behind him.

"Elle!" Ice yelled from inside the house. "What was that?"

"Gunfire," she answered her husband. Her eyes darted to Snow. "Shit, you're hit."

He let go of Jennifer, leaving her to lie on the ground as he sat back. He touched his head, feeling his fingers slide over a throbbing wound alongside his temple. When he looked, the unmistakable stain of blue covered his fingers. Blood.

"I don't think it's that bad," Elle said, grabbing a handful of snow and placing it firmly to his head so he could heal faster. "Hold that."

"Why would they shoot at me while I held Jennifer?" he asked. "She is one of them."

"They don't have the same loyalty that you

do." Elle frowned. "If they're taking shots, that means they're done trying to capture you."

"They want us dead?"

"They probably figured a dead or wounded alien is better than no alien at all, as far as a scientific study is concerned." Elle reached to open the car door. The overhead light came on. "Slide her onto the seat. It's the best we can do right now to keep her safe."

"I can run her inside," Snow said.

"You'd be too exposed." Elle pulled Jennifer's shoulders off the ground and started maneuvering her inside. Snow helped lift her. They shut her inside.

The forest was quiet. Snow pulled Elle down when she tried to look. "I will distract them. Get into the house."

The cabin door opened, and Meg lobbed the blaster at them before closing it. Snow reached for it.

"What are we going to do with that toy?" Elle dismissed. "I need a rifle."

Snow pressed a button on the side of the blaster and a small panel lifted on the back. He held it up to see who was in the forest. Yellow lines appeared where the blaster detected humanoids. "There are three of them."

"I take the toy comment back." Elle grabbed the device from him. "Okay, this is what we're going to do. We—*What the hell just happened?*"

Snow looked at the screen. Three had become two, then two's indicator line collapsed into a dot and turned orange. Two became one.

Panic filled him. His brothers hadn't yelled out in a while. They must have gone around to fight.

"My brothers must be in the forest." Snow instantly went to help them take down the attackers. "Keep Jennifer safe."

"Wait, then why aren't they showing on the —" Elle's words were cut off as he ran toward the last attacker.

"Snow," Ice yelled behind him.

Snow registered his brother's voice, but it was too late to back down. He charged into the trees, weaving back and forth in case they fired at him. He ducked behind some brush and listened. The forest was still quiet. He stayed low to the ground as he neared where the last shooter should be hiding. He found him crumpled on the ground.

"Hey, Snow." Gary smiled, lifting his hand as

he stood by the man. The alien had his human disguise partly on. The tough yellow flesh of his oversized head never really fit the head mask quite right. "You rang?"

"No." Snow stated. "I don't have bells."

"Then one of your brothers," Gary said. "We were in the neighborhood and thought to offer our assistance."

"What neighborhood? This is a forest." Snow eyed the man on the ground. The human was dressed all in black and had a gun.

"I am trying to learn American colloquialisms," Gary answered. "How has it been hanging? To the left?"

"I have not hung anything." Snow picked up the man's gun and walked back toward the car with it. He heard Gary stumbling behind him. Seeing Elle, he gave her the Earth weapon. "Here."

Elle took it and used the blaster to search the trees, checking for others. "Are they dead?"

"No," Gary answered. "But we did wipe their memories, so they will no longer be a problem. Corporate decided it was best we implement what you humans would call a clean slate initiative. They will be just like teenagers."

Elle did a double take when she saw Gary.

"Three grown men with amnesia. That won't be suspicious at all," Elle said dryly.

The alien lifted his hand in greeting. "Hello, Elle, how is it hanging with you?"

"Uh, it's hanging," she managed to answer.

Gary went to peek in the car. "You have a human in here."

"That is Dr. Petals. She works for Milano," Elle answered. "Can you clean slate her, too?"

"No," Snow put forth, not wanting them to hurt Jennifer. If they took her memory, she would not remember meeting him. Then again, maybe on some level that was a good thing, but he didn't want to be out of her memories.

"Petals." Gary tapped on the window a couple of times. "I like that name. Very much an Earth name. I will have to remember that for our next grooms—Petals, Flowers, and Hamburger. Very strong and manly, yet sensitive."

"How many more are in the forest?" Elle asked.

"Only ten, maybe thirty," Gary answered.

"Ten to thirty?" Elle demanded. "Can you narrow that answer a bit? Are we dealing with a mercenary team or an army?"

"Yes." Gary tapped on the window again.

"Which one?" Elle asked.

"Hello, little sleepy Petals. No, not sleepy. Angry." Gary swiped the blaster from Elle. He opened the door and shot it. "There you go."

"Dammit, Gary, where are the men in the forest?" Elle demanded.

"Oh, *this* forest." Gary made a strange clicking noise. "None. We got them. Well, except for those five dots about ten miles down the road."

"Elle?" Ice yelled. "Are you all right?"

"Gary's here," Elle shouted back. "You can come out now. We need to leave."

Ice stepped onto the porch, only to rush down to hold Elle against his chest. "I am glad you are unharmed.

Snow tapped his brother's arm. "We should go."

"I'll drive," Gary announced as he climbed into the driver's seat. "I know just where to take us."

## 5

Jennifer blinked, opening her eyes to a flashing neon-pink light. It took her a moment to focus. A heavy rock beat pounded through speakers, the sound too clean to be a live band. Her vision blurred, and her tongue felt thick and heavy. She smacked her lips a few times. It was not unlike a hangover.

It had been a while since she'd gotten one of those. She frowned. In fact, it had been a long while since she'd been drunk. Working for Milano required she had a clear head at all times. Living a lie wasn't easy.

Her hand pushed against vinyl, and she slid up in her seat. The dark nook was covered and shoved back into a secluded corner of the bar.

"Welcome to Your Lucky Night." A woman in a rhinestone bikini and high heels approached the table. "What can I get you? Scotch, fuzzy nipple, sexy sunrise, buxom blonde, bubbly brunette, randy red—"

Jennifer moaned and leaned forward on the table to see her surroundings. She wasn't just in a bar. She was in a strip club. Half-naked ladies danced onstage.

"What the...?" Jennifer rubbed her eyes.

"Not your thing? I'm sorry, but the men only dance on Thursday nights." The waitress stepped in front of her, blocking her view of the stage. "Your costume party already left, if that's who you are looking for."

"Left?" Jennifer slid around the table and got out of the booth.

"Yes, they told me to give you a few minutes and then see if you needed anything. I admit, I saw you all alone with no drink and thought I'd come sooner." The woman gave a small pose as she held her tray. The gesture was practiced.

"They just left?" Jennifer thought of Snow. What in the hell had happened? One minute they were in the cabin attacking her, and the next she's alone in a...nudie bar?

The waitress pointed toward the doors and said, "Yeah, just a—"

Jennifer didn't wait for her to finish as she ran toward the exit. None of this made sense. Where was her brother? Where was Snow?

A security guard started to stand at her swift departure, but the waitress shouted, "It's fine, Thunder."

Thunder stepped back, out of her way. "Have a nice day, ma'am."

Day?

She pushed through the doors and was greeted with sunlight. The narrow parking lot was situated between two tall buildings.

Seeing a flash of blue disappear around the back of an SUV, she chased Snow down. She caught up to him as he was about to get into the back seat of a car.

"What the hell?" Jennifer demanded.

"Shit," Elle mumbled under her breath. "I knew we should have blasted her again."

Meg and Frost sat in the back seat. Ice held the passenger door open for Elle.

"Three times was enough," Ice said.

"You shot me three times?" Jennifer looked down to check her body as she remembered being hit with some kind of electrical charge before passing out. There were no visible signs of the attacks.

"You were beginning to wake up, and they did not wish for you to." Snow smiled at her. "This must be fate. Meg said if we were meant to be together then you would find me again, and you have."

"That's not exactly what I said," Meg tried to interrupt.

In the light, the blue of Snow's eyes seemed to glow. For the briefest moment, she forgot what she was doing. His nearness did something to her, deep inside, causing her thoughts to fumble.

"You, ah..." Jennifer took a deep breath, regaining her ire. "You left me in a strip club?"

"Consider yourself lucky. I wanted to leave you on the side of the road," Elle drawled. "Gary recommended this place."

"Oh, shut up, already," Jennifer snapped. "You have no idea who I am or what you're talking about. Just because you saw your first alien a few months ago and decided it was love, doesn't make you special. Get over yourself. I've known aliens were real since I was a little girl."

To Jennifer's credit, Elle kept her mouth shut.

Someone honked the horn and yelled, "Asses in the seats, wheels on the road!"

"I don't think that's a real saying," Meg said.

"Heard it at a truck stop," the driver answered.

Jennifer leaned down, only to find a yellow alien whose skin looked like the back end of an elephant. He sat forward on the seat, close to the steering wheel so his legs could reach the pedals. Large black eyes blinked at her in rapid succession. "Hi, I'm Gary."

"He is correct," Ice said. "We need to find a place to hide."

"I have a place," Jennifer offered.

"In a Milano cage?" Elle snorted. "No thanks."

"An alien safe house," Jennifer said. "Do you think these three are the first aliens Milano has been after?"

"Well, yeah," Elle answered. "Everyone said..."

"Everyone who? Dr. Hanklen?" Jennifer gave a sarcastic laugh. "Yeah, he's known for his honesty and integrity."

"There are others, in other facilities?" Snow asked.

"Not anymore. Milano has had an unfortunate run of bad luck when it has come to capturing and keeping aliens." Jennifer watched another car pull into the lot. The man driving made no attempt to hide that he was staring at them through his window. "Do you want my help or not?"

"Yes," Snow answered.

"No," Elle said at the same time.

"Safe house?" Ice asked.

"Yes, a safe house. I need to call my brother," Jennifer said. "Do you have a cellphone I can use?"

"Yes." Snow pulled open the door to the back seat for her. Jennifer slid into the car and found herself pressed next to Frost as Snow sat beside her. Elle sat next to Mr. Yellow, and Ice next to her. There was barely enough room.

"Meg, lift up," Frost said quietly. Meg sat on his lap, freeing more of the seat.

Jennifer shivered as the two brothers cast off a chill. For many reasons, she was not in for a comfortable ride.

"I don't like this," Elle stated to no one in particular. "We should leave her."

"Would you like to lift up?" Snow offered.

If she wasn't mistaken, he looked hopeful that she'd climb onto his lap. Tingling started where their arms touched. The only reason she'd sit on him was for things she didn't want his family to witness. The fact she'd even thought something so sexual caused her to cough. "Um, no, no, I'm good. No."

It was too late. The image was in her head. Her eyes strayed to his hands and then moved up his forearm. How long had it been since she'd had sex? The answer didn't readily come to her.

"I need a phone," Jennifer said, desperate to take her mind off her wanton thoughts.

"We got this covered," Elle said by way of refusal.

"Road trip," Gary yelled. He backed up the car and then slammed it into gear, causing the tires to peel out on the parking lot asphalt.

Jennifer clenched her teeth and gripped her knees as her body rocked back and forth. Their driver drifted from his lane, took corners too fast, and made a strange clicking noise each time he had to use the brakes. She waited for the sound of police sirens. They never came.

"Can I borrow the phone, please?" Jennifer

glanced up at Snow. "I need to let my brother know I'm all right."

Elle turned around in her seat. Her eyes met Jennifer's before glancing downward. Automatically, Jennifer looked to see it wasn't her knee she was squeezing. It was Snow's. She snatched her hand away from him. She could tell by the woman's expression they were not going to be handing her a cellphone anytime soon.

"Where are we?" Jennifer asked.

"Earth," Gary answered.

"About two hours outside of Rumble," Meg said.

"Thank you." Jennifer gave the woman a slight nod.

"What did you mean when you said you've known aliens were real since you were a kid?" Meg asked. "Were you abducted?"

Jennifer's first reaction was not to answer. She wasn't used to revealing personal information.

A hand covered hers and Snow slid her fingers back onto his leg. She didn't look down but could tell he'd placed it higher than it had been before. A tiny vibration hit against her palm. She slowly slid her hand back to her own lap. The last thing she needed was to think about what his vibrations meant.

Seeing Meg still stared at her expectantly, she finally decided to speak. If she didn't at least try to build some kind of rapport with these people, she wouldn't be getting them to safety anytime soon.

"No, I wasn't abducted. I've never been on a spaceship," Jennifer said.

"Then what?" Meg prompted.

"We..." She drew the word out as she tried to form the sentence. "We lived next to one. We called him Harry. When my parents were indisposed, he took care of us."

"Us?" Meg asked.

"My brother and I."

"I didn't know you had a brother," Elle said, facing forward.

Snow again pulled her hand onto his thigh. She felt him leaning into her a little.

"You don't know everything." Jennifer snatched her hand back. "Jim is my twin."

"How were your parents indisposed? Did they work a lot?" Meg's questions were starting to feel like an interrogation.

"Yeah, something like that," Jennifer said.

"Something like what?" Meg prodded.

"My mother drank too much. My father worked too much," Jennifer said.

"What kind of alien was Harry?" Snow asked, giving her the excuse she needed to look in his direction. The bright blue of his gaze made it hard to concentrate. "Bevlon—"

"Bevlon?" Gary interrupted. "Are you certain? Did he try to eat you?"

"Bevlon-Angelion. Why would he eat me?" Jennifer frowned, insulted for her childhood friend. Harry had taken care of them, often feeding them when her mother forgot. Sure, he looked demonic with red skin and black eyes, but he'd been the kindest man she'd ever known.

Gary clicked before saying, "Bevlon-Angelion? That can't be right. Those two hate each other."

"Which is probably why he left home when he was the age for pain conditioning," Jennifer said.

"You are in love with Harry?" Snow asked. Was that a tinge of jealousy in his tone? She couldn't be sure, but he was studying her intently.

"He was like a father to me," she said.

"If this is true, and I'm not saying I believe it —" Elle started.

"I believe it." Snow talked over the woman.

"—but if this is true, then how could you work for Milano knowing what they are?" Elle finished.

"I work for them *because* I know what they are." Jennifer sighed in frustration. She felt accusation and distrust from all angles but one. Snow leaned a little closer to her, his leg pressing up against hers. "What better way to know your enemy than to go to work with them all day?"

"Is there any reason you can find to trust her?" Ice asked his wife.

Elle lowered her head for a moment. Finally, she said, "There did seem to be a lot of animosity between you and Dr. Hanklen. And you are known to be..."

"What?" Jennifer prompted when Elle didn't finish. The woman wasn't exactly one to mince words.

"A giant bitch," Elle said.

"What a coincidence," Jennifer quipped, "so were you."

The car fell into silence. Jennifer wasn't sure there was anything she could say to convince them of her sincerity, and she was still a little too groggy from being blasted to try.

## 6

SNOW HEARD THE OTHERS TALKING BUT found it difficult to concentrate on the plans they were making. Sitting next to Jennifer, especially after she'd grabbed his leg in an obvious attempt to show she was interested in him as a mate, had to be the most agonizingly pleasurable experience of his life. It was all he could do to keep his body from vibrating for the four Earth hours they were in the car.

"Almost there," Gary announced.

"Like we were almost there an hour ago?" Meg asked.

"No, closer than that," Gary said. He had put the radio on a crackly station where the music popped in and out of hearing. His head bobbed, pausing each time the music gave out.

Snow found himself staring at Jennifer's thighs. "Are you frightened?"

Jennifer turned to him in surprise at the question. "Of what?"

"Going on a spaceship." Snow let his finger slide against her leg in a soft caress.

Meg and Frost both witnessed the touch, but Snow didn't care. His brothers were always kissing and hugging their wives. Why shouldn't Snow do the same with his new woman?

Jennifer leaned forward, forcing him to meet her gaze. "A spaceship? No one said anything about a spaceship. I thought you had a safe house lined up."

"Nothing safer than my house," Gary piped in.

"Debatable," Frost mumbled.

"With Galaxy Alien Mail Order Brides, you are in competent—" Gary jerked the car to the side, taking it off-road for a few feet before righting it once more. "Squirrel."

Jennifer's hand gripped his thigh again, hard. Snow's breathing deepened. The car bounced as they turned onto a dirt road leading through the trees.

"Did he just call us incompetent?" Jennifer whispered.

Snow grinned, his mind focused on her touch. "His intentions are good."

"The road to hell..." Jennifer muttered as she leaned over him to look out the window. Her head angled as if she tried to see the sky.

"No. It is the road to the spaceship," Snow corrected.

"It's an Earth saying," Meg explained. "The road to hell is paved with good intentions."

"Sounds nice." Frost nuzzled his wife's throat. "Perhaps we should go. I would like to meet good people."

Elle turned around in her seat to look at Frost. "It's hotter than the sun."

"Oh, it's in the Solarus Quadrant," Gary interrupted. He started to turn around, letting go of the wheel so he could talk.

"No," Ice called out, leaning over to steer.

"Gary, drive," Snow ordered. He would not have him wrecking and risking his chance with Jennifer.

Gary didn't appear to register he'd done anything wrong as he again took the wheel. "We picked up a few passengers living in Solarus Quadrant on one of our first trips. Is hell the human word for Frxsolis? Lovely city. I didn't go inside, but I hear good things."

"Yeah, it's exactly the same thing," Elle answered.

"We can't go there," Ice said. "Sorry, my love. Those temperatures will kill us."

"I'd much rather see heaven anyway," Elle answered.

"Where is heaven?" Ice asked.

Elle moved to face her husband and kissed him. "Right here, my love."

Jennifer shifted in her seat, and Snow found her still gazing out of the window at the sky, away from the couples. He wondered what could be more interesting than watching people in love.

"Does your planet look like ours?" she asked, her words soft as if they were only for him, their own private discussion like a real couple. He liked that.

Jennifer's head was close to his. He leaned in and closed his eyes. Her hair smelled almost like the flowery stuff Meg kept in her bathroom. He liked that about her as well.

"It is called Sintaz," Frost answered, breaking into their private conversation.

Snow opened his eyes, only to see his brother gesturing that he should talk. His thoughts raced with desire, and he wasn't sure what he should say. Jennifer angled her head, nearly touching the glass as she looked upward.

"It looks like a ball of ice." Meg directed her eyes toward Jennifer's back a couple of times, pausing to look at him between glances. "Or so I've been told."

Frost tried to lean over to see what Meg looked at.

Meg shook her head to stop him and mouthed to Snow, *Talk to her.*

"I am tired of trees," Snow stated. It was true. The forest was so isolating and lonely. Animals ran from him. People did not cross his path. It reminded him of Sintaz—desolate, empty, and a little sad.

Jennifer's hand lightly brushed his, and he held his breath. Their eyes met. She was so close he could have easily kissed her. His lips twitched a little as if trying to reach her. The warmth of her breath hit his jaw.

"Oh, sorry, I didn't mean to..." Jennifer pulled

away as if realizing she leaned over his lap. "I was looking...for..."

"Spaceships?" Meg supplied.

Jennifer gave a little nod.

"We don't have trees on Sintaz." Frost's eyes were wide as he nudged the discussion to continue. "I find them interesting."

"What do you like about Earth?" Jennifer asked.

"You," Snow answered honestly.

She blinked a few times. "Oh, uh..."

"Just go with it," Meg said. "They're always that blunt."

"Thank you?" Jennifer's tone was strange and a little breathy. Each time the car bounced it rubbed their legs and arms together. The sensation stimulated his already amorous body. He knew he was vibrating, but he couldn't help it. The reaction was as natural and uncontrollable as his beating hearts.

"You are welcome." Snow nodded once. The car swayed as Gary took a series of curves a little too quickly.

"Do you like anything about the planet?" Jennifer prompted.

"I liked working in Colorado Springs when

we first arrived. The area was mountainous. If I was to stay here..." Snow felt his two hearts begin to pound. Could he stay? He was looking at a very compelling reason to.

She appeared surprised at his selection. "I remember we were tracking you to that area when you were...first..."

"When you and the rest of Milano were hunting us down?" Elle inserted.

"I thought we were past the accusation part of the car ride. Did you ever wonder how it was you managed to make it out of the desert facility?" Jennifer asked. "Do you honestly think it was all talent and dumb luck?"

"Well, yes," Elle answered.

"How about when the lockdown initiated the exact same moment you made your way out of the main complex and into the carport? Or how the main gate didn't close until right after you drove through?" Jennifer continued.

"You assisted us?" Ice asked.

"You were lucky I was in the security room and could distract the guard to give you time to get free." Jennifer leaned forward and reached for the passenger seat near Ice's shoulder. "I am sorry, Ice, for what you were put through. I want you to know that I contaminated all of your samples. They will not be attempting to clone you anytime soon."

"Are they cloning?" Meg asked.

"Not yet, but it's on the company's wish list. They've been trying to recruit geneticists." Jennifer fell back against the seat. Her attention once again turned to him.

"I have to ask, what job did you have in Colorado Springs?" Meg questioned. "I don't think you ever told me."

Snow grinned. "I was muscle."

Jennifer glanced at his chest, and her breath caught.

"I don't understand," Meg said.

"When people did not pay their bills, I was sent to collect their payments." Snow couldn't look away from her. The car slowed.

"You were a bill collector?" Meg arched a brow.

"Yes. A man would make a bet, then lose, and then not pay his bill, and I would go and make him pay it or punish him. It seems to be an honorable enough system to keep people honest." Snow sighed. "It was an easy job. I do not know why more humans do not do it."

"Um, Snow, sweetie, I think you were a thug who worked for a bookie," Meg explained.

"I am your sweetie," Frost broke in. "You cannot also marry my brother."

"You better be teasing," Meg answered, "because I only have eyes for you."

"I have all parts for you," Frost said. The couple began to kiss, and Jennifer leaned closer to Snow, averting her gaze.

"I was called an enforcer, not a thug." Snow hoped Jennifer could see that he could provide a good, honest life for a mate. "They gave me cash to enforce the bill collecting. I can hunt for food too."

"You hunted your..." Jennifer leaned away from him.

"Two separate things." Meg chuckled. "He means he can earn money, and he can hunt for food to provide for you."

"Oh, that's nice?" Jennifer did not sound convinced.

"Welcome to the Sintazian courtship," Meg said.

"Almost there," Gary called.

"Like we were almost there thirty minutes ago?" Meg replied dryly.

"No, the ship's right here." Gary pulled the car to a stop by an empty field. "Or it will be once night falls."

"Thank goodness," Meg said, "I need to stretch my legs."

"Oh, yeah, me too. I need out of this car," Elle agreed.

Meg and Ice opened their doors to exit the vehicle. Snow placed his hand on Jennifer's thigh to stop her and felt heat radiating from between her legs. "Can we have Earth sex now?"

Jennifer made a small choking noise. Her voice sounded funny when she said, "I think I need to stretch my legs, too." She slid out of the car behind Frost.

Snow frowned, even as he opened his door.

"Well done," Gary told him, clicking rapidly. "I think she likes you. If you two mate that means we have a perfect record and can go back to corporate without shame."

Snow paused, not exiting. "What do you mean you can go back?"

"I don't think I said that."

"Gary." Snow stiffened. "You're going to tell me what you mean by that."

Gary rocked back and forth, a low tone sounding from within him.

"If you want to get back on your ship, you're going to tell me." Snow would not follow through with the threat, but Gary didn't need to know that. "Do you *need* me to mate to Jennifer?"

Gary's words came out in a panicked rush. "Galaxy Alien Mail Order Brides is not pleased with our performance. We convinced them Earth was the best territory to expand the bridal procurement agency. All the data said it was a sure thing. We took the grooms to the marriage town, Las Vegas, where women come to get married to strangers. We gave them all strong names. But a group of grooms went rogue when they stole a stripper bus, and then a Killian was arrested for attacking an ice cream cart, and then a few of the grooms put women in their suitcases and tried to smuggle them onboard. Corporate wanted to take our ship, but we convinced them we could make it work and..."

"And?"

"We found you and your brothers. You seemed not to have a lot of options or family, and we thought it was an easy sell. We did not expect you to take so long or be so picky. Nothing went as we planned," Gary finished.

"Are you telling me that if you don't get us mated, you're out of a job?" Snow verified. "Is that why you kept asking my brothers to do your hologram testimonials? Is that why you keep coming back to help us?"

"Would you do the testimonials? That would be wonderful. We can have a holobox ready to record the second we get on the ship. How long do you think it will take you to mate to Jennifer?"

"How long do you think it will take you to stop Milano?" Snow countered.

"Do I hear the ship?" Gary reached for the door and got out of the car.

Snow followed him. The alien tried to hurry away, but his short stride was no match for Snow's.

"What is happening?" Ice called after him.

"Snow?" Frost yelled.

Snow stepped in front of Gary, blocking his escape to the nearby trees. There was no ship trying to land. "Tell them."

"Tell us what?" Frost asked. The women ran toward them.

"They can't stop Milano," Snow stated. "All

their promises are worthless. We can't stay on Earth without being hunted."

"That's not what I said," Gary protested.

"Do the lies never end?" Frost demanded.

"Our extensive research has shown that most Earth women react favorably toward relationships when they are threatened." Gary tried to back away, but Frost and Ice helped circle around the alien so he was contained.

"That logic sounds flawed." Jennifer joined them. "What were the parameters of your research?"

"Movies." Gary swayed on his feet and clicked.

"Movies?" Jennifer repeated in disbelief.

"Yes, so we would know how best to help the grooms mate with women in the fastest way possible." Gary tried to edge one direction and then another. He was blocked from escaping the conversation.

"Watching movies is hardly an acceptable method of determining real human interactions. It's only valuable in a study of the cultural effects movies have on society, and vice versa." Jennifer sighed. "Am I to understand that you have been bringing aliens to this planet, trying to play match-maker, based on movies?"

"Action movies. We enjoy the transmission waves we pick up in this airspace." Gary clicked, and it sounded like laughter. "It does get in the way of work sometimes. Like when we didn't see the beacon going off because we found a particu-larly clear reception and...oh, right, that was your beacon. Forget I said that. I can assure you we have logged well over three thousand Earth hours on our research efforts. First, there is the danger. Then, there is the kissing. Last, there is a list of names to indicate they are happy together and there is no more story to tell."

"Holy crap, you all hitched a ride with idiots," Jennifer muttered. "No wonder your initial landing was so easy to track."

"We adjusted our—" Gary protested.

Snow lifted his hand to stop him from contin-uing. "What about Milano?"

"He is on his way to Minnesota," Jennifer said. All eyes turned to her. Snow moved closer to her. "He wants to—"

The sound of a gunshot cut off her words and, seconds later, heat struck Snow's arm.

He grabbed Jennifer and thrust her into the

center of the circle they'd made around Gary, blocking her from the gunfire. Elle protested as Ice shoved her next to Jennifer. Meg went a little more willingly into the cluster. Within seconds, the brothers surrounded them like a shield and began rushing them toward the nearby trees.

A second shot sounded, echoing through the trees.

Snow swept Jennifer into his arms and continued to run toward cover. She made a weak noise and clutched his shoulders. A third shot resulted in a loud crack as car windows shattered.

"They must be tracking us," Elle said. She looked accusingly at Jennifer.

"It's not me. I don't have anything on me," Jennifer answered. "It's probably the car. It wouldn't have been hard to slip a tracker on it while you dumped me in a strip club. You know better than most how much tech Milano's teams have at their disposal."

"Did you see where the shot came from?" Ice asked as they found shelter crouching behind the trees.

Snow set Jennifer on her feet and pointed to where the shot had come from.

"You're bleeding." Jennifer grabbed his arm.

Snow glanced down, unconcerned.

Meg grabbed snow from the ground and pressed it to the wound. "Is everyone else all right? Did anyone get hit?"

The ache in his arm lessened with the cold.

"Hold this," Meg said. Jennifer took over caring for him.

"Where's Gary?" Elle asked. "Did they get him?"

Snow leaned to get a visual of the field. The path to the car was clear. "I don't see him."

"Does anyone know where we are?" Meg whispered.

"Middle of nowhere," Elle answered. "Did anyone grab the bag out of the car?"

Everyone shook their heads in denial.

"Then we have no weapons," Elle said. "Shit. We're sitting ducks."

Snow put his hand over Jennifer's as the snow began to drip down. "I will do everything I can to protect you."

"This isn't your fault," she answered. "None of this is."

"Please do not leave me." Snow pulled her hand away from his wound. Her fingers were chilled, and he brought them to his chest. With the cold, his body warmed a little. "Fate brought you to me twice."

It was true, first in the forest, and then when he'd allowed the others to put her in the naked-dancer bar for safety. Jennifer pulled her hand out of his grasp and grabbed another handful of snow to press to his arm.

"Let's survive this and then worry about fate," she said.

## 7

Sabotaging lab samples and helping aliens escape captivity made for a stressful life. Jennifer constantly worried about getting caught. She had been apprehensive about being alone with a bunch of aggressive alpha male mercenary types. She'd dreaded whenever Dr. Hanklen walked into a room.

None of that compared to the fear churning inside her now. They were trapped in a forest surrounded by armed mercenaries of an unknown number. The car was in the clearing, so close, yet too far to run to.

Maybe she could make it. Maybe they wouldn't shoot her, the esteemed Dr. Petals. Out of all of them, her going made the most sense.

Jennifer took a deep breath. She could make it. Adrenaline would give her speed.

*One. Two.*

Jennifer tensed—and nearly screamed as Elle grabbed her arm. In her heightened state, the contact caused her heart to leap wildly in her chest.

"Thank you," Elle whispered.

"For what?" Jennifer wasn't sure how to react. How did the woman know she planned to run for the car?

"For helping us escape the desert facility," Elle answered. "I didn't know you had done that, but it makes sense that we would have had help."

It was a little weird to be thanked regarding a conversation they'd had while driving, but Jennifer nodded in acceptance, knowing it had taken a lot for a woman like Elle to say the words. "You're welcome."

"We should go deeper into the woods," Frost said. "Maybe we will find shelter or help."

"We don't know what is out there," Ice countered.

Jennifer felt Snow's gaze on her. His nearness made her feel brave. He and his brothers had faced so much to come to Earth, and for the hope of finding love. How could she fault them for that? In many ways it was such a noble goal, much more so than hunting aliens to do scientific experiments on in hopes of some advancement. Dr. Hanklen didn't even know what he was looking for. He just looked.

Jennifer took a deep breath and stood. She stepped into the clearing with her hands lifted.

The car engine revved to life, stalling her movements. Before she could make it more than two paces, something heavy hit her back.

She fell forward. Snow had knocked her over and landed to her side to shield her body.

"Snow, get her back here," Meg called.

Jennifer struggled. "Let me do this. I can make it to—"

The sound of the car broke through her plea as she realized someone was driving toward them. She pushed up, pulling Snow to come with her. The car wove before the back end swung to the side, skidding around to a stop in front of them.

A shot rang out, then another. More glass shattered.

"Get in," Gary ordered.

Snow reached for the back door, opening it before tugging Jennifer toward it and forcing her inside—not that she would have protested the rescue. Snow slid toward her on the seat, then Meg and Frost. Snow pulled her head down toward his lap and leaned over her. The cocoon of his body kept her from seeing anything but the space between his legs.

"Go!" Elle yelled.

The car rocked violently. Jennifer held her breath and closed her eyes, waiting for more gunfire. She bounced and slid along with Snow. It felt like a long time before the vehicle seemed to take a straight path. Snow eased his hold on her, and she managed to peek up.

"Are you hurt?" he asked, cupping her cheek. She could see the concern he had for her.

Jennifer's hands shook, and he took them in his.

"I don't think so," she answered.

"Do you see why letting Milano chase us is a bad idea, Gary?" Snow's voice rose in anger. "Your attempts at matchmaking are going to get everyone killed."

"There may be a reason to reevaluate our methods," Gary allowed. "I can see that now."

Wind whipped through the car from the broken windows. Jennifer pushed her hair back and held it in her fist to keep it from her face. The colder the car became, the warmer Snow felt next to her. She leaned into him. He wrapped his arm around her and held her to his chest.

No one spoke. Frost angled his body to watch the road behind them. Snow gazed out of the window beside her. Ice kept watch over the other side. The brothers seemed to have a natural way about them, one she'd observed in small behaviors every time they were together. They acted like a unit, each moving in seamless harmony with the others; demonstrated when they'd circled around them after the first gunshot, the way they surveyed their surroundings now.

"Faster," Frost said, prompting the others to look behind them.

Jennifer saw glimpses of a car chasing them, but it disappeared from view as their driver wildly jerked the vehicle back and forth. She felt Snow's weight shift beside her. His eyes had turned forward.

A dark shadow fell over the interior of the car. She followed his gaze.

A metal craft hovered in the air, its vast body blocking the light. At their approach, it began to lower to the ground.

Knowing spaceships were real and seeing one firsthand were two entirely different things. This was no pointed rocket ship humans launched into orbit, nor was it like the flying saucers seen in alien hoax videos. Instead, it reminded her of an industrial snowflake. Pieces of metal protruded at odd angles, but with an overall symmetry when taken as a whole.

"That's..." Jennifer tried to say spaceship, but the word caught in her throat and all she could manage was a small gasp of air.

"Everyone, get ready to run," Elle ordered.

"No need." Gary stepped on the gas, heading straight at the ship.

Jennifer instantly reached to grab hold of Snow. Her hands fisted in his clothes and held on tight as if he were the only thing keeping her grounded.

"Gary?" Meg asked, only to repeat herself with growing panic. "Gary!"

"Sh-it." Elle groaned, bracing her hands on the dashboard like that could stop her from flying through the broken windshield when they crashed.

In this cosmic game of chicken, a car would surely lose to a spaceship.

"Turn the wheel," Jennifer whispered, wishing her voice was louder. "Turn the—"

Gary listened, slamming the wheel hard to the right. It sent their back-end skidding. His course correction came too late, and Jennifer saw the side of the ship coming toward her window. She let out a scream and kicked the door so that she was thrust into Snow in a fruitless effort to escape impact.

The ship lurched, and just as they almost crashed, a narrow door opened and swallowed the car into its depths.

The whistling wind abruptly stopped. A loud clank threw them into total darkness. Gary turned off the engine, and the sound of heavy breathing echoed around her.

The overhead dome light switched on, and she watched Gary step out of the car. The dim light cast over the area. Gary disappeared into the darkness.

"What the...?" Elle whispered before giving a nervous laugh. The sound triggered a response in Meg, and she too began to laugh.

"Omigod," Meg exclaimed.

"I can't believe we freaking made it," Elle

added. A couple of clanks made it sound as if gunshots had hit the side of the ship.

An overhead light switched on to reveal the cargo area. Jennifer stayed plastered to Snow's side as the others exited the car.

Meg held out a cellphone toward her. "Oh, hey, Jennifer, I was going to let you borrow this back at the clearing before, well...you should call your brother. I know how important family is."

Jennifer disentangled her fingers from Snow's clothing and accepted the phone with a shaky hand. "Thank you."

Meg nodded.

"Jennifer?" Snow cupped her chin and drew her face up so he could study her.

"I've never been shot at before," she said. Her mind raced, and she had a hard time holding on to her thoughts. "Or crashed into a spaceship."

"It's all right."

"I don't like heights." That old fear tried to creep in, but her body was already pushed to the brink.

"Do you feel that vibration?" His gaze didn't leave hers. "That's the engines engaging. Next, it will rock as we leave the ground. After that, a few jolts and bumps then it's smooth flying. It will feel just like standing on the planet."

Jennifer wasn't sure what prompted her to lean forward, but she pressed her lips to his and kissed him.

The touch was brief. When she pulled away, his lips were pursed and his eyes remained closed. She took the invitation and kissed him again. This time, longer. Her lips parted, moving desperately as she sought more of his comfort.

"What did I tell you? See, action movies. Give her a little danger, a little gunfire, a little car chase —it's like an Earth woman aphrodisiac." Gary's voice barely registered.

"Let's give them a little privacy," Ice said. "You know Earth women don't like it when we watch."

## 8

JENNIFER WASN'T SURE WHAT CAME OVER HER. She felt a dam break inside her, flooding her with emotions and desires she couldn't control. As a scientist, she knew the effects that adrenaline had on a human body. The passion pouring through her blood couldn't be attributed to just that. There was more than the gasping of her breath, the pounding of her heart, and the shaking in her limbs.

She was pulled toward Snow by an invisible force. It was counterintuitive to everything she knew as an academic, and yet there it was. She was drawn to him. From the moment he'd found her spying on his family in the woods, she'd wanted him. The attraction was undeniable.

With each movement of their mouths, the kiss deepened, and she didn't want it to stop. She shrugged out of her coat for better mobility. He smelled of the fresh autumn air, of nature right before the first snowflakes fell. His skin remained warm after the cold drive to get to the ship.

The ship jerked just as he said it would, and she pressed her hand to the seat to catch herself. A shard of glass pierced her palm, and she yelped in surprise. The wound didn't hurt as she lifted her hand. Snow reached to pluck the shard from her skin.

"There is a medical device that can help that," he said.

"It's fine." Jennifer stopped him from leaving the car. She glanced around the cargo area, seeing the others had left them alone. She pulled off her shirt and wound it over her hand to keep the blood from smearing. It was more material than she needed but was the only bandage she could think of at the moment. Then, she swiped at the seat to knock any remaining glass onto the floor.

Snow's eyes focused on her bra, and he reached for her breasts slowly. A hand cupped each mound, and he squeezed softly. "I have always wanted to touch these."

It took everything for Jennifer to suppress a surprised laugh.

He hooked his fingers on the top edge of lacy material and pulled the cups down so he could further explore. He pushed at her nipples like buttons. His bright blue eyes focused on her chest. As much as she would like to let him continue his exploration, her heart was beating too fast, and she needed more.

Snow's body vibrated, pulsing with a steady rhythm from between his thighs. The sound was hypnotic and primal. She softly moaned as she leaned into him.

Her lips parted before they met his in a deep kiss. No thoughts came to her beyond needing him. She pulled at his shirt, wanting it off of him. He leaned away to undress. Jennifer watched him disrobe as she fumbled to unbutton her pants.

Strong muscles bulged beneath his blue flesh. Her eyes went to his lap as he pushed the jeans down his hips to reveal his naked cock. She expected a moment of fear but found herself fascinated instead. His erection stood tall from his hips. Though generally shaped like a human male's, the tip was narrower and small beads vibrated beneath the skin.

Snow reached for her sex and pressed his hand against her wet pussy. "My brothers tell me I will fit in here."

She gasped as he pushed his fingers into her and began probing around. Her body quaked, and if he would have rubbed her clit harder, she might have come right then and there.

"Do all Earth woman have hair here? I have never seen such a thing," he said.

"Mm, yeah." She nodded, breathing harder.

He grinned. "Yes. This softness will do nicely. I should like to put myself in there now."

Jennifer wrapped her fingers around his vibrating shaft. He moaned at her touch.

"Please," he begged, "give me the moving-Earth sex. Show me."

The plea was too much. She pushed up from the seat. His fingers slipped out of her. Jennifer straddled his lap and drew the tip of his blue penis to her sex. It tickled and teased as he vibrated her. She lowered herself onto him.

Pleasure like she had never known erupted within her. The pressure of her body on his caused the vibrations to intensify.

He leaned forward to lick a nipple, enthralled with her breasts. "Everything about you is soft."

Jennifer braced her hands on his shoulders and lifted slowly, only to press back down. She rocked her hips in shallow thrusts. His eyes lifted to meet hers, and he held her gaze.

There were things she felt she needed to say, but she couldn't think of a one. Every nerve sang with need and building pleasure. Her muscles tensed. The vibrations intensified, stimulating all the right spots.

"I have never felt anything like this," he whispered.

"Neither have I." Jennifer moaned as she kissed him.

Snow matched her rhythm thrust for thrust. Jennifer could hardly believe this was happening. No Earthling had ever made her feel the way this alien did. In that moment, she knew she had been waiting for him her entire life. They were meant to be together.

Snow was right. It was fate. He'd traveled across the universe to get to her.

Tremors started inside her sex, only to pour throughout her entire body. Snow gripped her by the hips, holding her down on his lap. She stiffened, unable to cry out as the pleasure overcame her. His shaft pulsed inside her, sending a shock-wave of electricity through her as energy flowed out of him and infused her with heat.

Jennifer breathed hard. She blinked several times, trying to focus her thoughts. As her climax settled, she remembered where they were—the back seat of a damaged car in the cargo hold of an alien ship.

She'd had sex with an alien.

In a car.

On a spaceship.

An alien spaceship.

"We..." She swallowed, lifting off him to sit next to him. She leaned on her hip and grabbed her underwear. She pulled the panties on, so she wasn't bare-assed on the seat.

Jennifer righted her bra. Though she couldn't see anyone in the room that didn't mean they weren't being watched somehow. She leaned toward the window and glanced along the ceiling. There were many protrusions, globes, and hooks, but their functions were unclear.

"We?" Snow asked, still naked beside her. His vibrating body had settled to a low hum.

"What?" Jennifer glanced at him.

"You said we," he answered.

"I don't remember what I was going to say." Jennifer found her wadded shirt on the seat and pulled it on. It had fallen off her hand during intercourse and dots of blood stained the side. The euphoria of sex and adrenaline began to wear off, leaving her in an uncertain aftermath.

*We are in space.*

*We're in a spaceship.*

*We had sex.*

*We didn't talk about what that means.*

*I think I'm falling for you. Hard.*

Jennifer said none of the thoughts rolling through her mind. She gathered the rest of her clothing and stepped out of the car. The metal floor of the cargo area had a rough texture. She made quick work of pulling on her jeans.

"What is wrong?" Snow asked. He hadn't bothered to start dressing as he also came out of the car. "I do not know how to interpret this expression on your face. Did I do something wrong? This was my first time with the Earth sex, and Sintazians normally do not move the hips—"

"No, no." Jennifer reached to touch his shoulder in reassurance. "You did everything right. I was just thinking...thoughts."

"Thinking thoughts?" he questioned. "Is this a colloquialism?"

"No, it's me rambling." She gave a small laugh. "I have a thousand thoughts in my head."

"What are these thoughts you are rambling?" Snow appeared concerned.

Jennifer took a deep breath. "I'm worried because we're in space. I want to see because how often do humans get to go to space, but at the same time, I'm afraid I'll have a panic attack and pass out because you can't get much higher than space. I'm trying not to think about it, but the more I try not to, the more I do."

Realizing she was talking emphatically with her shaking hands, she forced them to her side. She shifted her bare feet on the rough floor.

"I'm also worried about Milano. I don't see how we'll ever stop them from coming after us," she said.

"Us?" Snow sighed and appeared to relax. He remained naked and made no move to change that. "Is it only the threat that gives your face that expression? I worried you had rambling thoughts about our being together."

"I like being with you." Jennifer moved around him. She leaned into the car to grab her socks and boots, sitting on the edge of the seat to pull them on.

"And I like being with you." Snow reached in to touch her.

Jennifer saw the cellphone Meg had given her to use on the floor. She dodged his hand as she moved to pick it up. "Shit."

A wave of guilt crashed over her. How could she have forgotten? Normally, she was conscientious and precise. What was happening to her?

She again got out of the car as she looked at the phone. No signal.

"What is it?" Snow asked.

She lifted the phone to show him. "My brother."

His brow furrowed as if he didn't understand.

"Jim, my brother. He hasn't heard from me for hours and will be worried. When I met you in the forest, he was on his way to pick all of us up and move you to a safe place where Milano couldn't find you." Both Jennifer and her brother knew the dangers they had signed up for, but that didn't make them worry any less.

"Come. You can call him from the cockpit." He began to walk away.

"Wait, shouldn't you put something on first?"

She couldn't help glancing at his firm, bare ass. Desire began unfurling in her once more.

Snow looked down and chuckled as he went to gather his clothing. "I keep forgetting how modest Earth women are."

## 9

Space looked a hell of a lot more infinite when floating in the middle of it. Jennifer expected nausea and dizziness as she looked out of the viewing screen at her home planet. Instead, she felt peace. All the stress and danger was all rolled up on that one tiny spot. If she pressed her fingers to the viewing screen in the hallway, she could blot it from view entirely.

"Jennifer? Are you frightened?" Snow's hand on her shoulder gave her comfort. It felt natural that he should stand so close.

"No." Jennifer lifted the cellphone to check for a signal. It showed a couple of bars, but when she redialed the number to try Jim yet again, the call didn't go through. "Can we try the cockpit?

You said they might be able to help me get a call through."

"Of course." Snow slid his hand onto the small of her back and guided her down the corridor. The viewing screen automatically closed as if sensing their departure.

The corridors were long and metal, with strips of light going down the side of the wall to illuminate the way. The grates on the floor showed tubing beneath with green liquid running through it. There was so much technology that she didn't know what to ask about first.

Feeling the phone in her hand, she asked about none of it. Calling Jim had to be her priority.

Snow quickly walked as he led her through the corridor to the cockpit. The area was larger than any spaceship she'd seen pictures of. Gary sat in front of a panel of buttons and lights. Small dots of light with the ghosted images of tree tops showed on what looked to be a radar device.

"Gary, I need to call—" Jennifer began.

"This is Bob," Snow said.

"Oh, ah, I'm sorry," Jennifer apologized. Looking at the yellow alien, she wasn't sure she could tell the difference between him and Gary. "Bob, I'm Jennifer. I need to use your phone."

"She needs a signal boost," Snow said.

Bob pushed several buttons. "Signal is a go."

"Thank you." Jennifer tapped Jim's number in the recent call log on the cellphone and held it to her ear. The cockpit started ringing. She frowned. "Wait, what's happening?"

"Hello." Jim's voice was strained.

"Jim?" She wasn't sure if she needed to hold the phone to her mouth or not.

"Speak louder," Snow said.

"Jim, it's me," Jennifer said, louder.

"Jenny? Thank goodness you're all right," Jim said. "Where are you?"

She stiffened and grabbed hold of Snow's arm for support. Jim knew she'd hated to be called Jenny ever since they were kids. He'd only do it if he were in trouble.

"Where I said I'd be. Where are you?" she asked, unsure what she should say.

"She knows." Dr. Hanklen's voice came through the intercom. Louder, he continued, "Dr. Petals."

"How can I help you, Doctor?" she asked, gripping Snow tighter.

"You've been a busy girl," Hanklen said.

"I like to keep active." She closed her eyes and took a deep breath. "How can I help you? I don't suppose you took Jim's phone just to chat."

"You mean your brother?" Hanklen asked. "I wonder why you never mentioned him before."

"Jim, are you all right?" Jennifer couldn't keep up the pretense. A muffled sound answered her. "What are you doing to him?"

"Just keeping him company." The voice was familiar, but she didn't automatically place it. Was it one of the mercenaries she'd worked with at the desert facility? "Why don't you join us? Bring your new friends."

"What new friends?" It was a weak attempt at protecting Snow, and she knew it, but she had to try something.

She heard a scuffle, and then her brother grunted. Jennifer closed her eyes, trying not to picture what they were doing to her brother.

"We know you sabotaged the lab samples," Hanklen asserted. "I couldn't figure out why they kept degrading so quickly. And, as much as we hate recording what we do in the lab, I made an exception. We have you on surveillance. We also know you helped blue-one-six escape."

"This is about me, not Jim. Let my brother go, and I'll take his place. You can tell me all about your wild accusations."

"Jenn, no!" Jim yelled. A loud smack followed the sound.

"No," Snow stated.

Jennifer motioned at him to be quiet.

"Who do you have with you?" the familiar voice asked. "Is that the alien?"

"What's going—" Elle appeared behind her.

Jennifer spun around and held up the phone. She pressed her finger to her lips for silence.

"Tell you what," the familiar man continued. "You bring the aliens to me, then you and your brother can go about your way. I'll even throw in a nice severance package."

"Jenn, don't listen—" Again, a smacking sound cut off her brother's words. Jennifer jumped a little at the sound.

"Is that Milano?" Elle whispered.

Jennifer nodded, recognizing the familiar voice now that Elle said it. She'd only met the man a couple of times in passing but had heard him on television.

Shit. Milano and Hanklen had her brother. Hanklen was terrifying enough on his own.

Franky "The Heart Attack" Milano wouldn't get his hands dirty, but that didn't mean he couldn't have them all killed with one wave of his checkbook.

"I don't have them," Jennifer said.

"I think if you look around that ship hard enough you can find them," Milano answered. Of course he knew about the ship. His men had chased them onto it.

A tear slipped over her cheek. Jim was the only family she had left. People always said twins had a strong bond. She believed it. Every time they hit her brother, she felt like someone had punched her in the gut.

Snow cupped her cheek and said softly, "I am an acceptable trade. Let us get your brother."

Jennifer made a soft sound of disagreement. She tried to press her fingers to his mouth to quiet him. He kissed the tips before taking her hand in his. Her eyes narrowed as she gave a shake of her head.

"Where are you?" Elle asked when Jennifer didn't answer.

Bob clicked and pointed at the radar before giving what looked to be an alien thumbs-up. He knew where her brother was. The thought gave her little relief. She knew what these men were capable of.

"We'll meet somewhere public," Jennifer said. "Me for Jim. That's the exchange—"

The sound of Jim's cry of pain cut off her words.

"Leave him alone!" Jennifer yelled.

"I'll text you coordinates to this number, and you let me know how long it will take for you to get there. But don't make us wait long," Hanklen warned. "Bring the alien or your brother's dead."

"Don't you dare hurt—" Jennifer started to threaten.

"Communications off," Bob said.

Jennifer let out a weak cry, and her legs gave out from under her. Snow caught her before she fell, holding her up as he hugged her close.

"What did I get us into? Jim, I'm so sorry," she whispered, wishing her brother could somehow hear her. Hot tears slid down her cheeks.

"I'm getting really tired of these assholes," Elle said. "Bob, it's past time. No more games. No more action-movie bullshit. If you know how to take these jerks down, do it."

"But..." Bob looked at Jennifer and Snow.

"I'll do your testimonial. Just end this. No more games," Snow said.

"So you're mated?" Bob asked.

"No," Snow said.

"Yes," Jennifer answered at the same time. She looked up at him. Her emotions were all over the place, but in a world of chaos, that one answer felt right.

"Yes," Snow amended.

Bob clicked excitedly before pushing a button to announce over the intercom system, "We have optimal mating. One hundred percent success. Well done, crew, on this mission!"

"Crew?" Elle asked. "Isn't it just you and Gary?"

"I knew our plan was a good one. Earth women better get ready. We're bringing you men!" Bob bounced back and forth.

Snow released her, pausing to make sure she was steady before placing his hand on Bob's head to stop him. "First, we save Jennifer's brother and take down Milano for good, or there will be no more missions to Earth."

Bob blinked rapidly and made a strange noise before turning back to the control panel. Lights began to flicker.

"We have incoming coordinates," Bob said. "Adjusting our flight path and scanning the area."

"Answer them," Snow said, "but give us time to make a plan."

"Tell them we're driving there," Jennifer added. "No need to let them know we're arriving there by spaceship."

"They'll believe that," Elle agreed. "They wouldn't expect the aliens to risk their mothership."

"I need to speak to my brothers," Snow stated.

"We need to come up with a good plan because sacrificing you or your family to save mine isn't an option. I already know what Jim would say to that plan." Jennifer's whole body shook, and she didn't know if she should cry or scream.

"I know this isn't the best time." Elle stopped her as she tried to follow Snow out of the cockpit. "But, congratulations on your marriage."

"Marriage?" Jennifer repeated.

"Sintazian custom. You have sex, you say you want each other, that's pretty much the wedding in a nutshell," Elle said. "Simple and abrupt."

"How do you know we had sex?" Jennifer asked in surprise.

Elle gave her a look that said everyone knew. "Come on. Let's rescue your brother and kick everyone who works for Milano in the balls once and for all."

The woman was crass at times, but Jennifer didn't disagree with the sentiment as she followed her apparent husband down the corridor. She couldn't think about all that now though. Jim needed her.

## 10

SNOW WOULD DO ANYTHING FOR HIS WIFE. Anything. Even if that thing was sacrificing himself to save her brother.

The moment she'd said she wanted him, everything in his life made sense. The expression on her face as Milano and Hanklen tortured her brother would forever haunt him. He never wanted her to feel that fear again.

"I must do this," Snow told his brothers. "She is my wife, and she needs her brother."

Ice and Frost nodded in understanding.

"Then we all do it," Frost said.

"Yes, we'll all go," Ice agreed.

Snow expected no less from them.

Elle and Meg spoke with Jennifer. He hoped

they were saying things to comfort her, to calm her fears, and to lighten her heart. As humans, maybe they had the ability to say things in a way that would help. Though the metal room, round lights, and numerous grates looked normal to him, he watched as Jennifer's eyes kept darting around.

Seats filled the passenger deck, shaped in anticipation for several species. They formed a circular pattern, some seats long and narrow, others with three half circles molded into the seats. It indicated the ship catered to more than humanoid couples. All that was missing was a tank full of slime to transport Lophibians.

The welcome message shimmered from alien language to alien language on the wall, "Welcome to Galaxy Alien Mail Order Brides, where we are joining hearts across the universes." He only read that much because of the Earth upload they'd given him. Before, it had been a lot of gibberish. No one ever translated messages for Sintazians.

Galaxy Brides kept that promise. His hearts were joined to Jennifer's heart.

"We're going with you," Elle stated, drawing his attention away from the shimmering message.

"Where?" Snow asked.

"No," Ice stated, apparently already under-standing the statement.

"That's adorable when you think you can order me around, but yes, we're coming with you to face Milano." Elle lifted on her toes to kiss her husband.

That is what she meant? There was no way they could allow the women to be put in danger yet again.

"No," Snow agreed with Ice. "They want us. We will go and protect you."

"He's my brother." Jennifer came before him and placed her hand on his chest. "I'm going."

"You are my wife. I must keep you safe and happy." The word *wife* came out of his mouth so easily, and yet it hung in the air between them. It was the first time he'd said that to her, and part of him was afraid she'd deny it, that he'd misunder-stood what had happened in the cockpit.

"Yes, and as my husband, I expect you to respect me. Jim is my brother. You are my husband. And," her words hesitated as she looked at Ice and Frost, "this is my family now."

The last statement didn't sound as confident as the first two. If it had only been Jennifer and her brother, he could understand how having a new family might feel overwhelming.

"I do respect you," Snow said. "But I don't see how that is relevant when it comes to protecting you."

"Meg, at least tell me you are staying to..." Frost began, only to let his words trail off as Meg arched a brow in his direction.

"They're expecting me," Jennifer said. "I have no choice. But you do. You don't have to do this." She turned to his brothers. "Any of you. If something was to happen..."

Ice and Frost both crossed their arms over their chests and stared at her.

"Yeah," Elle drawled. "I already told her not to bother trying to change your minds."

"We are going," Ice stated.

"You are our sister," Frost added. "That makes Jim our brother."

"There is no question," Snow said, his tone final.

Tears filled Jennifer's eyes as she nodded. "Thank you."

"Now that it's settled, we need a plan," Elle said. "I don't know about the rest of you, but I'm sure as hell tired of Milano and his nonsense."

## 11

"I don't like this. There are too many of them, and we're exposed," Jennifer whispered as she walked next to Snow. She knew his brothers, along with Elle and Meg, watched them, but she hardly felt secure in the plan they'd hatched. Mainly, because that plan depended on Gary and Bob coming through, and by all accounts that duo was beyond incompetent. "And of course, it would have to be dark and in the middle of nowhere."

"You should return to the spaceship," Snow said. "I will go alone."

It was not the first time he'd made the suggestion, so she didn't bother answering it again.

"Are you sure the ship is safe where it is?" she asked, also not for the first time. "Sorry, I know you already said it was cloaked and Milano's people wouldn't detect it. I'm nervous, and my head keeps going down this strange checklist of concerns."

"I will not let anything happen to you." Snow sounded like he believed that, but she couldn't be sure. He might not have a choice.

The snow had melted on the narrow gravel road during the day, only to freeze as the temperatures dropped to create patches of ice. She wove around them while trying to keep up with Snow's longer stride.

"Two dozen men is a lot." She kept her voice low as she tried to examine their situation. "How many do you think Bob and Gary can reach with their clean-slate thing? Two? Four? So that leaves twenty. A handful will be scientists on standby— three for each of you, just in case they get lucky. So that makes eleven. Minus Milano if he is here, and Hanklen. Leaves roughly nine armed mercenaries?"

"Only nine?" Snow nodded. "That is not so many."

"I should have called my brother sooner. Maybe I could have—" she began.

Suddenly, he held out his hand in front of her.

She nearly crashed into it as she was focused on watching the ground. "We're here."

Jennifer looked around at the quiet road. Though open fields were on either side, they were blocked by narrow rows of trees. She leaned closer to him and whispered, "How do you know?"

"The smell is unmistakable." He looked surprised she couldn't detect it.

Jennifer leaned her chin down and inhaled. Snow smelled of autumn leaves, and she found it soothing. But she never stopped to wonder if humans gave off an odor that was unpleasant to Sintazians.

"Elle said it was the bluing that some of the men put on their weapons," he explained. "We do not like the smell, but it does give away their position."

"Ready?" Jennifer took a deep breath.

Snow nodded. "Yes."

"I should probably tell you I love you, just in case something bad happens," she whispered. Snow reached for her, but she stepped in front of him and tilted her head back to yell, "Hanklen. Let's do this already! And don't try anything funny. We have laser beams from space aimed right at your ass, and the two dozen men with you."

The part about the laser beams wasn't true, but it sounded like it could be. The idea that someone might fire a shot at any moment circled in her brain, and it took everything for her to stay standing. Her legs trembled, and she had to ball her hands into fists. She felt Snow's fingers lightly touch her back. That small gesture gave her comfort.

"Dr. Petals," Hanklen called. "I'm surprised you came. I almost wagered that you'd run away like the treacherous coward you are."

Jennifer swallowed nervously, willing her voice to be strong. "Enough pleasantries. Where is my brother?"

"Safe enough for now," Hanklen said. "It looks like you're traveling light. Where are the other two specimens?"

"In a location that you won't find without me. All I want is my brother. You give me him, and as soon as we are free, I'll give you the information you want." Jennifer stiffened as she felt Snow come closer to her back. It took everything not to fall against him for support. She blinked away the tears that tried to fill her eyes.

"They talk as if I can't hear them," Snow grumbled. "Like I am an animal."

"You and your brothers were smart. When you were held, you didn't say much. Hanklen is convinced you have minor speaking skills but have not mastered the language." Jennifer stepped to the side. She tried to stay in front of Snow.

Their standard tranq darts wouldn't affect Snow, but the new TRQ-30 she had used on him worked to knock him unconscious. If Hanklen had weaponized it...

She pushed the thought from her mind. She needed to concentrate. Her heart pounded with fear.

She couldn't lose Snow.

She couldn't lose Jim.

Jennifer didn't want to be here, but she had no choice. All she had ever wanted was to do good, to save aliens from a horrific fate, to pay Harry back in some small way for taking care of two latchkey human kids with a tough home life. She'd known her path was dangerous, but part of her had refused to admit just *how* dangerous.

She detected movement in the shadows ahead, and Jim stumbled forward. His hands were bound. He landed on his knees before trying to stand.

Jennifer automatically went toward her brother. Instinct fueled her movements. He was alive and within reach.

A shot was fired, causing her to skid to a stop before she even made it close. Her hands lifted to her sides. She looked at Jim. Her brother still moved. She turned to look at Snow. Her husband stood beside her.

Snow pushed her behind him, shielding her with his body.

Another shot sounded, this one farther away. It was answered by three more. Jennifer grabbed Snow's arm. "What's happening?"

## 12

"Edur? Izotz?" Snow called to his brothers in their native language. "What is happening? Where are you?"

"Snow, I need to go..." Jennifer wrapped her fingers around his biceps and tried to move around him. He refused to let her slip in front of him. He put his arm around her and held her close to his side while he angled his body toward the man struggling to his feet on the road. "That's Jim!"

"We can't rush," Snow said, tightening his hold when she tried to force herself free. In a sterner voice, he repeated, "Jennifer, you can't rush into danger. We must use caution."

She stopped struggling. He didn't dare take

his eyes away from the end of the road, but he felt a hot liquid drip onto his arm. He would do anything to take away her tears.

The only reason he's agreed to her coming was because Elle pulled him aside and warned him that Jennifer might never forgive him if he didn't. He was familiar with the strength of Sintazian women, so that didn't surprise him, but Jennifer was much more delicate in form than his people.

There was so much he didn't understand about Earth women and their customs. He should have risked her wrath to keep her safe. Then he would have a lifetime of begging forgiveness.

Three men stepped behind Jim. One was clearly a mercenary, with his gun and superior build. The other two wore dress shirts, like they'd been interrupted from a fancy party.

"Milano," Jennifer whispered, "and the taller one is Hanklen."

"We must walk now," Snow said. "Are your weakened legs better?"

Jennifer didn't answer as she pulled away from him. She took a step. Her head was lifted and her face unreadable, but he knew she wasn't all right.

"Dr. Petals," Milano said. "Good to see you again."

Even if he weren't the diabolical boss of a corrupt foundation, Snow would have wanted to hit him. He wasn't sure what the right human word was for the impression Milano gave, and that brief ponderance caused his mind to begin running through a list of words.

*Smug. Foul. Sleazy. Smarmy. Arrogant—argh, stop.*

Stupid language uploads. It had been a while since they'd tried to unpack a rush of knowledge into his brain. There couldn't have been a worse time. He blinked hard, forcing himself to concentrate as echoes of words whispered through his thoughts.

"Send my brother to me," Jennifer said.

Milano reached into his jacket and shook his head. He pulled out a gun. "No. I don't think I will."

"Jim," Jennifer yelled.

Snow darted forward, not caring what happened to him.

"Snow," she screamed.

Milano blinked in surprise as if he hadn't

expected Snow to charge at him. He moved his weapon from pointing at Jim to aiming it at him.

Milano fired, and the shot missed.

The mercenary reached for his weapon—only to scream as a halo of light encircled his head. He fell to his knees, grabbing his temples.

Hanklen turned in horror at the sound. He tried to run, but Ice came from the trees to block the doctor's path.

Milano swung his gun toward Ice, but Frost appeared behind the man, causing him to turn in the other direction. Snow leapt forward and swung the heel of his palm at Milano's jaw. He made contact, snapping the man's head back. Milano's gun fired into the air as he flew backward.

Snow followed him down, seizing hold of the gun hand and squeezing tight. He heard a bone crack and loosened his grip. Milano dropped the weapon. He yelled for help. Snow punched the man's face with his palm, shutting him up.

"Jim, what did they do to you?" Jennifer said behind him.

Snow glanced around to make sure all threats were handled. He pinned Milano to the ground. Ice held Dr. Hanklen around the neck. Elle had hold of one of the doctor's wrists. Meg scurried forward to grab Milano's gun from the ground. Frost stood over him.

The mercenary lay on the ground, unmoving. Gary approached him, holding a small device in his hand, which he flipped into the air and then caught. "You, sir, have been clean slated."

"The others?" Snow asked.

"Taken care of," Ice said. "There are only these two left to deal with."

"You were able to take out nearly two dozen people on your own?" Jennifer asked. She sat on the ground by her brother, her arm around his shoulders.

"Not us." Ice pointed at Gary. "Bob and Gary zapped them."

"Won't remember a thing," Gary said. He again flipped the device in the air, only to drop it on the ground when he tried to catch it. He scrambled after it, crawling as it rolled away from him.

"What do you want to do with these two?" Meg asked. She held the gun pinched between her fingers and walked it over to Elle. "Take this."

Elle complied. "I want to shoot them."

Milano groaned and began kicking his feet. Snow pinned his arms as the man thrashed.

"Clean slate them," Meg said.

Gary reemerged. He leaned over to pat at Milano's jacket before pulling out a phone.

"Can we decide? I would like to be done touching him now," Snow said. All he wanted was to hold his wife in his arms, and for this finally to be over.

"Just one moment," Gary moved to Milano's broken hand and pressed a digit to the phone to unlock it. Then, he noisily clicked as he tapped his yellow fingers rapidly against the surface.

*"Millionaire businessman, Franky Milano, is in hot water this evening after several videos from anonymous sources appeared all over the internet. What some initially thought was a hoax has now caught the attention of the FBI,"* a woman with a serious voice said from the phone.

*"That's right, Susan, and I don't think anyone at the Federal Bureau is laughing at these serious allegations of money laundering, racketeering, tax evasion and, get this, using government grant money to fund a secret extraterrestrial research facility in Nevada,"* a male voice answered.

*"Beam me up, Steve,"* Susan said with a laugh. *"I guess the Milano nut didn't fall far from the*

*family tree. His grandfather was notorious for his ramblings about alien abductions.*"

"What...?" Milano stared at his phone.

"Did you leak videos?" Meg reached to take the phone from Gary.

"Part one of the plan to take down Milano," Bob said as he joined them. "Part two is to take away his funds, which we have diverted through a series of intricate networks. Our Earth research shows that men of power lose that power without money or reputation."

Milano's phone beeped. Meg laughed and looked down at Milano. "Um, looks like your senator friend just disinvited you to lunch next week." Another beep sounded. "And golf is canceled. Looks like everyone is distancing themselves from you."

"You have no idea who you are messing with," Milano said.

"Shut up, Frank," Hanklen ordered.

Elle pointed the gun at him. "Shut up, Hanklen."

"You can't do this. I'll be ruined." Milano's voice was caught between anger and fear.

"Told you we had a plan," Gary said. "We just

had to wait until the action worked its magic and found mates for all of you."

"One hundred percent success," Bob said to Gary as if congratulating him on a job well done. They both began to click.

"Take them," Jennifer said.

Snow nodded at Milano while looking at Frost. His brother instantly took over subduing the man as he hauled him to his feet.

Snow turned to his wife and her brother. Jim had been beaten, but he was upright and standing without assistance. As he approached, Jim flinched and tried to protect Jennifer.

"No, Jim, it's all right." Jennifer went to Snow and wrapped her arms around him. "I was so scared. I thought they were going to shoot you."

"Look at this thing," Elle said, gesturing to her gun hand. "It's a relic, and not a very well maintained one at that. You probably couldn't hit the broad side of a barn with this thing. Why is it rich idiots always think paying more for something makes them cool? Only a dumbass would bring a weapon like this to a fight."

"I—" Milano began.

"No more talking." Frost shook him hard.

"What are you going to do with us?" Hanklen asked.

"What did you mean by take them?" Snow asked his wife.

"Bob and Gary should put them in a cage and take them to space. It seems poetic. That's what they wanted to do to aliens. Now they can see how it feels. We can't let them go. Milano, even if we erase him, is still Milano, and will have allies. Odds are he'll eventually figure out what happened to his money, and what he'd been doing with it, especially if there are clues from those videos that were released. Same with Hanklen. A doctor as opinionated and as widely published as he is would draw serious attention if he were to show up brain wiped."

"I guess we could always sell them to a Kintok trader," Bob said, unsure. "They won't fetch a good price though."

"No," Snow denied. "Drop them off some-where they can do no harm, but do not cause harm to come to them."

"Don't you guys have an ice hut you're not using?" Elle mused.

"You can't do this," Hanklen denied.

"Hey, does anyone have one of those blaster

things? They're giving me a headache," Jennifer said.

"Oo, can I do it?" Elle asked. "I haven't had a chance to fire it yet."

"One blaster, coming up," Bob said.

Jennifer took Snow by the hand and led him to her brother. "Snow, this is my brother. Jim, this is Snow. My husband."

Jim started to laugh, only to catch himself. "Husband?"

"You are now my brother," Snow said, holding his hand out. "Welcome to my family."

"Uh, yeah." Jim reached forward to shake it. "You were right, sis, these guys' body temperatures are—"

"We can talk about all of this on the ship," Jennifer interrupted. "Right now, I just want to get out of here."

"As you wish," Snow said. "Bob, bring the ship. I want to take my wife home."

13

EPILOGUE

Jᴇɴɴɪғᴇʀ sᴛᴜᴅɪᴇᴅ ʜᴇʀ ʜᴜsʙᴀɴᴅ ғʀᴏᴍ ᴛʜᴇ couch as he leaned over a table with his brothers, including Jim, who all three Sintazians had adopted as their own. Apparently, Sintazians didn't have the same family hierarchy that Earth had. When you married, all of your family became all of their family. It was how ice clans stayed strong in the olden days on the frozen planet.

The four men whispered as if contemplating whatever was on the table with great severity. Christmas lights flashed, casting all of them in different colors.

"Hey, um, Jenn." Elle stood in the kitchen of

her parents' guest home, gazing at the tree. They had all been staying there since the final battle with Milano. Even though Bob and Gary swore the threats were gone, there was comfort in being cautious.

"Yeah?" Jennifer couldn't help watching her husband's ass.

"Come here a sec, would ya?" Elle motioned her over. Meg came from upstairs.

Jennifer grabbed her coffee mug to get a refill while she was in the kitchen and went to stand by Elle. "What?"

"Do you see anything different about the tree?" Elle asked.

Jennifer turned to see what Elle meant. All the round ornaments had been moved into groups of two, and smaller balls had been adhered to the larger ones.

Meg glanced at it and laughed.

"Are those supposed to...?" Jennifer didn't want to say it.

"Boobs," Meg supplied. "Our husbands paired up the Christmas ornaments to symbolize boobs."

Jennifer couldn't help herself as she started to laugh.

"What is so funny?" Jim asked, looking at the women in the kitchen.

"Please tell me you didn't have anything to do with the tree," Jennifer said.

"Nice, huh?" Jim grinned.

"No." Jennifer shook her head.

Snow smiled at her. "Jim brought us glue. We made Christmas boobies. He said hand-making ornaments is an Earth tradition."

Meg and Elle nearly lost it as they practically fell to the floor behind the counter to laugh.

"Nice, Jim." Jennifer shook her head at her brother.

"What?" Jim raised his hands as if he didn't understand her reprimand. "I'm helping them understand Earth ways just like you asked me to."

"What are you all looking at?" Jennifer moved to the table. A crude map had been drawn on a piece of paper. At the end of a trail, the word "Lair" had been written. "What is this?"

"We must prepare for the coming attacks," Frost said.

"Oh no." Meg's voice came from behind the counter. She poked her head up to look at them. "Not—"

"Santa's reign of terror must be stopped," Ice said.

"Our bodies can withstand the arctic temperatures. We must protect our new homeworld from the threat," Snow explained. "Jim said he would rent movies to help us prepare for battle against the elf army. There is a trilogy we are supposed to see."

Jim's look could best be described with the expression "shit-eating grin."

"We're going to set booby traps," Frost said.

"Santa may be evil, but he is a man," Jim inserted. "All men fall for a booby trap at one time or another."

"Jim," Jennifer scolded.

"We must protect our women," Snow insisted. He pulled her against him and kissed the tip of her nose. She felt a subtle vibration starting against her stomach. The man's attraction for her had not waned one bit.

"Jim, payback is going to be a bitch," Jennifer warned, even as she chuckled.

"So worth it." Jim went toward the kitchen. "We have any beers left?"

"I would love to continue to vibrate next to

you," Snow said, completely unashamed that everyone heard him.

Jim groaned, "Ugh, dude, we talked about that. She's my sister."

Snow ignored him as he continued, "But we must prepare. Christmas is a week away. We have to be ready. We need cookies to subdue him. And firewood. And socks."

"Stockings," Ice corrected.

"Yes, stockings filled with coal to hit him with," Snow said. "Don't worry, my love, I promise to keep you safe. No harm will ever come near you again."

Jennifer smiled at his sincerity and leaned up to kiss him. "I love you, Snow."

"And I you," he answered.

As the men went back to the table to resume their battle plans, Jennifer went to the coffeepot to refill her mug. She glanced at Elle.

"Don't look at me," Elle said. "Meg was supposed to explain it to them."

"What? I tried," Meg protested. "I think I was making headway until Jim decided to help."

Jennifer merely laughed. "I guess we can let them believe in the miracle of Santa for just one Christmas before we take their fun away."

"I think it could work," Snow said as Jennifer made her way back to the couch to gaze at the pretty lights on the boob tree. "Just like when we trapped bellaphants in the ice caves. No man is going to give my wife pointy ears."

The End

THE SERIES

## Galaxy Alien Mail Order Brides Series

Spark

Flame

Blaze

Ice

Frost

Snow

KEEP READING!

DETERMINED PRINCE

Captured by a Dragon-Shifter Book One

Dragon-shifter Prince Kyran has studied the Earth people and is ready to assimilate. Female shifters are all but going extinct on his planet of Qurilixen, and his people are desperate for mates—so much so they're taking matters into their own hands. What better place to capture a woman than Earth? After all, dragon-shifters had come from there centuries ago. Surely a human female would be honored to be selected by one as fine and fierce as himself?

While on Earth, Kyran stumbles upon the most beautiful woman he's ever imagined, singing something the natives call rock 'n' roll. His blood simmers and he knows Eve is the one for him. But taming this feisty female is going to take much more than his training prepared him for.

READING GUIDES

MICHELLE M. PILLOW NOVELS

## Free Reading Guides

Download free reading guides in MOBI or EPUB formats from MichellePillow.com.

# ABOUT THE AUTHOR

## *New York Times* & *USA TODAY* Bestselling Author

Michelle loves to travel and try new things, whether it's a paranormal investigation of an old Vaudeville Theatre or climbing Mayan temples in Belize. She believes life is an adventure fueled by copious amounts of coffee.

Newly relocated to the American South, Michelle is involved in various film and documentary projects with her talented director husband. She is mom to a fantastic artist. And she's managed by a dog and cat who make sure she's meeting her deadlines.

For the most part she can be found wearing pajama pants and working in her office. There may or may not be dancing. It's all part of the creative process.

## Come say hello! Michelle loves talking with readers on social media!

www.MichellePillow.com

facebook.com/AuthorMichellePillow

twitter.com/michellepillow

instagram.com/michellempillow

bookbub.com/authors/michelle-m-pillow

goodreads.com/Michelle_Pillow

amazon.com/author/michellepillow

youtube.com/michellepillow

pinterest.com/michellepillow

COMPLIMENTARY EXCERPTS

TRY BEFORE YOU BUY!

**Captured by a Dragon-Shifter Book One**

**Determined Prince
by Michelle M. Pillow**

Dragon-shifter Prince Kyran has studied the Earth people and is ready to assimilate. Female shifters are all but going extinct on his planet of Quril-ixen, and his people are desperate for mates—so much so they're taking matters into their own hands. What better place to capture a woman than Earth? After all, dragon-shifters had come from there centuries ago. Surely a human female would be honored to be selected by one as fine and fierce as himself?

While on Earth, Kyran stumbles upon the most beautiful woman he's ever imagined, singing something the natives call rock 'n' roll. His blood simmers and he knows Eve is the one for him. But taming this feisty female is going to take much more than his training prepared him for.

## Determined Prince First Chapter Excerpt

*Draig Northern Mountains, Planet of Qurilixen, the near future*

Prince Kyran adjusted the bandana around his neck as he peered deeper into the dark cave hidden within the mountain. At least, he was fairly sure the thing around his neck was called a bandana. Or was it a handkerchief? It was hard to remember all the human words. Technically, his people still spoke a dialect of an Earth language, but so much had changed in the centuries since they'd left the planet, that many new words and customs had to be learned.

"My name is Kyran. You look like an honorable woman," he whispered, practicing what he would say to any prospective mate. "I have a home with my parents and my brother. There we will live and you will be part of our family. Would you like to give me many children?"

Behind him, the mountain valley air was sweet, a blend of grasses and tiny blue flowers. It mixed with the almost acidic smell of porous black rocks now surrounding him. It wasn't the darkness that caused the tiny jolt of apprehension in his stomach. His shifter eyes could easily cut through the shadows. It was what awaited him beyond the dark stone walls—marriage.

Kyran smiled thoughtfully to himself, perhaps simple was best. "Come to my home planet and I will make you my princess."

The Draig, Kyran's people, were a race of dragon-shifters. Long ago, they'd escaped Earth, using a portal to come to a place where they could live out in the open, free of persecution. The Var, friends of the Draig people, had come with them. Vars were cat-shifters and had just as much reason to leave the old world. Only by working together had the two races managed to make a clean start. It was an alliance so strong that Kyran couldn't imagine it ever changing.

Perhaps he should try poetic. "You will like my planet. Qurilixen is a wondrous place bathed in almost constant daylight. In the valley near the borderlands, there is a forest of oversized trees—so big that from a distance the taller ones look like your castle homes on Earth. Here we will join and become one."

Though he'd never actually been to Earth himself, Kyran had seen pictures of the old palaces in the royal library, and they were very much like the castle he and his family lived in. Only some of the elders could actually remember making the trip across, and they had been little help as to what to expect. A few scouts had been through the portal to study modern Earth and to make sure the trip would be safe. They spoke of tall square castles and loud noises.

"This will be easy," he told himself in determination. "Earth has many women. Finding one will not be hard. I have studied the transmissions. I am ready for this assimilation into Earth culture. I am a fierce dragon and will make a fine husband. A woman would be lucky to have me. I will find a princess." Fear tried to work its way into his brain, but he pushed it aside. He had to stay determined.

This had to work—not only for him, but for his people.

Luckily, Earth had advanced to a state that humans aired transmissions. They called it television, and once the shifters had learned to capture those waves, they'd been able to study the new Earth culture to practice blending in.

"How-ow-dee-ee," he sounded out slowly, trying to mimic the wavy intonation of the customary greeting. He liked the cowmen. They appeared to be a tough breed of humans who spent much time outdoors riding funny looking ceffyls around open fields.

Blending was better than the royals' original plan of sneaking through the portal and kidnapping human women like the barbaric tribes written about in old scrolls. At least this way, they could get a good look at the females before they snatched them. To some, the idea seemed extreme —bringing women through the portal in order to marry them. It had taken decades before enough of the elders had finally agreed to the plan. Unfortunately, the Draig and Var no longer had a choice. If they didn't find compatible mates soon, their kind would die out in a generation. The few alien species who had made contact were not mating material for a number of reasons—incompatible biology, conflicting customs, no desire to live onworld.

For some reason, female shifters were no longer being born. The males thrived, growing stronger, living much longer than before. Couples had even been encouraged to have more babies to up the odds. Nothing worked. Now they had a large generation of men with little hope of marriage. Their best scholars were working on the problem, but until a solution was found, for the sake of their survival, they needed to find brides.

Historical documents indicated humans were reproductively compatible. This portal was their best hope, a way for the men of their planet to have a chance at happiness.

Their ancestors had caved in the portal when they'd first arrived on Qurilixen. Apparently, they'd thought no one would ever want to go back and wished to keep humans from following. Only after years of digging had the Draig unearthed it. Prince Kyran would be one of the first four grooms to go through. It was his duty to show the people this plan would work.

Many elders weren't happy with the plan to find mates this way, for they still carried the emotional scars from the old days. Human religions had changed, and with their new beliefs had come the idea that all shifters had made pacts with some person named Demon. If there were signed treaties with this Demon, any records had been lost.

Some shifters hoped time had changed the humans. Because of the controversy, the four princes had volunteered to go first and prove this could work. Prince Kyran and his younger brother, Prince Finn of the Draig, would join Princes Ivar and Rafe of the Var. It wasn't decreed which of them would come back with a bride, only that they had to start looking.

"Ready?" Finn asked, coming from behind Kyran carrying a torch. He glanced over Kyran's outfit and smirked.

"What?" Kyran looked down. He looked exactly like a cowman with boots, a hat and tight pants. Actually, he'd chosen the style of dress for the tight pants. What better way to show off one of his finer assets? "It's better than what you picked."

Finn grinned. He was dressed as a great warrior. "We shall see who turns the most heads, brother."

Hearing a noise, both dragon-shifters turned. Prince Ivar's green gaze glinted from the darkened shadows. When he stepped forward into the torchlight, he wore the native clothing of the cat-shifters. Fitted black pants pulled low across the hips, showing off a fair amount of stomach. The matching black shirt was laced down the center front, revealing a strip of his chest. Kyran quirked a brow.

Ivar waved a hand in dismissal. "The tailor brought me a gown and said I was to go to this accursed planet in it. I refused. I much rather receive stares than blend in as a woman—royal Earth custom or not. What is a *draqueen* anyway? It sounds like your ancestors, not mine, dragons."

Kyran shared a look with his brother. Finn shrugged. He didn't know either.

"Where's Rafe?" Kyran asked. "The portal's about to open."

"Here!" Prince Rafe called. His footfall sounded over the cave as he jogged forward. His white pants belled wide at the bottom, matching the white long-sleeved shirt. Rafe glanced at his brother's non-attire and said distractedly, "Sorry."

The more serious Ivar grunted. "You lost track of time before *this*?"

"I felt like someone was following me. I doubled back to the borderlands before returning," Rafe said. Then defensively, he added to Ivar, "You think I'm paranoid, but I'm telling you, not every Var wants to see us marry humans. Arguments are still being made that taking humans will dilute shifter blood and cause us to lose our natural abilities. They would rather take to the stars and meet other humanoid species or wait for the gods to bless us."

"It is not their place to question a Var royal decree," Ivar stated to his brother. "The elder council had their say. This will be."

"Shall we?" Kyran wanted to stop the two cat-shifter brothers before they began yelling. Moving to walk deeper into the cave, he glanced over his shoulder to see if the others followed.

"I don't know why you're so eager to meet your destiny, Kyran," Finn said.

"Aren't you?" Rafe asked. "I can't wait to find a bride to share my bed. The women ships don't come often enough for my taste."

"I've told you to stay away from those ships. You do not know what diseases the alien travelers carry in their profession," Ivar said.

"I only watch them dance," Rafe defended.

He let fur sprout over his nose as he made a face at his brother's back. Finn hid his laugh.

"What if you get a shrew?" Ivar sounded reasonable, like always.

"So long as she's shrewing in my bed, I don't care." Rafe winked.

Ivar grunted by way of an answer.

Kyran knew Rafe loved nothing more than to aggravate his stoic brother. "Come. The time is soon. Remember, only one is to find a bride this time. They want us to take it slowly."

"And I elect Kyran." Finn laughed, slapping his older brother's shoulder so hard Kyran stumbled. "This was his idea."

"Agreed," Rafe said quickly, not breaking stride.

Kyran opened his mouth as he righted himself, but Ivar had said, "Agreed," before he could get a word in. The three princes laughed. Kyran took a deep breath. He knew his duty, and if he must go first to ensure the future of his people, so be it.

"Ach! Come on then. Now is as good as later." Kyran forced a chuckle, not wanting to admit he was nervous. "So help me, when I'm finished you all had better go next. I'll not be the only prince settled."

**www.MichellePillow.com**

## Captured by a Dragon-Shifter Series

Determined Prince

Rebellious Prince

Stranded with the Cajun

Hunted by the Dragon

Mischievous Prince

Headstrong Prince

PILLOW FIGHTER FAN CLUB!

FAN OF MICHELLE M. PILLOW?

Want to join an awesome group of readers?
facebook.com/groups/MichellePillowFanClub

## PLEASE LEAVE A REVIEW
### THANK YOU FOR READING!

Please take a moment to share your thoughts by reviewing this book.

Be sure to check out Michelle's other titles at www.MichellePillow.com

Made in United States
North Haven, CT
19 November 2022